Fasting, Feasting

Fasting, Feasting

Anita Desai

Thorndike Press • Chivers Press
Thorndike, Maine USA   Bath, England

This Large Print edition is published by Thorndike Press, USA and by Chivers Press, England.

Published in 2000 in the U.S. by arrangement with Houghton Mifflin Company.

Published in 2000 in the U.K. by arrangement with Random House.

U.S. Hardcover 0-7862-2638-2 (Basic Series Edition)
U.K. Hardcover 0-7540-4239-1 (Chivers Large Print)
U.K. Softcover 0-7540-4240-5 (Camden Large Print)

The text of this Large Print edition is unabridged.
Other aspects of the book may vary from the original edition.

Set in 16 pt. Plantin by Anne Bradeen.

Printed in the United States on permanent paper.

British Library Cataloguing-in-Publication Data available

Library of Congress Cataloging-in-Publication Data

Desai, Anita, 1937–
    Fasting, feasting / Anita Desai.
        p. cm.
    ISBN 0-7862-2638-2 (lg. print : hc : alk. paper)
    1. East Indian students — Massachusetts —
Fiction. 2. Brothers and sisters — Fiction.
3. Massachusetts — Fiction. 4. Young women — Fiction.
5. India — Fiction. 6. Large type books. I. Title.
PR9499.3.D465 F3 2000b
  823′.914—dc21   00-037762

To those whose stories I've told

Part One

One

On the veranda overlooking the garden, the drive and the gate, they sit together on the creaking sofa-swing, suspended from its iron frame, dangling their legs so that the slippers on their feet hang loose. Before them, a low round table is covered with a faded cloth, embroidered in the centre with flowers. Behind them, a pedestal fan blows warm air at the backs of their heads and necks.

The cane mats, which hang from the arches of the veranda to keep out the sun and dust, are rolled up now. Pigeons sit upon the rolls, conversing tenderly, picking at ticks, fluttering. Pigeon droppings splatter the stone tiles below and feathers float torpidly through the air.

The parents sit, rhythmically swinging, back and forth. They could be asleep, dozing

— their eyes are hooded — but sometimes they speak.

'We are having fritters for tea today. Will that be enough? Or do you want sweets as well?'

'Yes, yes, yes — there must be sweets — must be sweets, too. Tell cook. Tell cook at once.'

'Uma! Uma!'

'Uma must tell cook —'

'È, Uma!'

Uma comes to the door where she stands fretting. 'Why are you shouting?'

'Go and tell cook —'

'But you told me to do up the parcel so it's ready when Justice Dutt's son comes to take it. I'm tying it up now.'

'Yes, yes, yes, make up the parcel — must be ready, must be ready when Justice Dutt's son comes. What are we sending Arun? What are we sending him?'

'Tea. Shawl —'

'Shawl? Shawl?'

'Yes, the shawl Mama bought —'

'Mama bought? Mama bought?'

Uma twists her shoulders in impatience. 'That brown shawl Mama bought in Kashmir Emporium for Arun, Papa.'

'Brown shawl from Kashmir Emporium?'

'Yes, Papa, yes. In case Arun is cold in

10

America. Let me go and finish packing it now or it won't be ready when Justice Dutt's son comes for it. Then we'll have to send it by post.'

'Post? Post? No, no, no. Very costly, too costly. No point in that if Justice Dutt's son is going to America. Get the parcel ready for him to take. Get it ready, Uma.'

'First go and tell cook, Uma. Tell cook fritters will not be enough. Papa wants sweets.'

'Sweets also?'

'Yes, must be sweets. Then come back and take dictation. Take down a letter for Arun. Justice Dutt's son can take it with him. When is he leaving for America?'

'Now you want me to write a letter? When I am busy packing a parcel for Arun?'

'Oh, oh, oh, parcel for Arun. Yes, yes, make up the parcel. Must be ready. Ready for Justice Dutt's son.'

Uma flounces off, her grey hair frazzled, her myopic eyes glaring behind her spectacles, muttering under her breath. The parents, momentarily agitated upon their swing by the sudden invasion of ideas — sweets, parcel, letter, sweets — settle back to their slow, rhythmic swinging. They look out upon the shimmering heat of the afternoon as if the tray with tea, with sweets, with fritters,

11

will materialise and come swimming out of it
— to their rescue. With increasing impatience, they swing and swing.

⚭

MamandPapa. MamaPapa. PapaMama.
It was hard to believe they had ever had separate existences, that they had been separate
entities and not MamaPapa in one breath.
Yet Mama had been born to a merchant
family in the city of Kanpur and lived in the
bosom of her enormous family till at sixteen
she married Papa. Papa, in Patna, the son of
a tax inspector with one burning ambition,
to give his son the best available education,
had won prizes at school meanwhile, played
tennis as a young man, trained for the bar
and eventually built up a solid practice. This
much the children learnt chiefly from old
photographs, framed certificates, tarnished
medals and the conversation of visiting relatives. MamaPapa themselves rarely spoke of
a time when they were not one. The few anecdotes they related separately acquired
great significance because of their rarity,
their singularity.

Mama said, 'In my day, girls in the family
were not given sweets, nuts, good things to
eat. If something special had been bought in

the market, like sweets or nuts, it was given to the boys in the family. But ours was not such an orthodox home that our mother and aunts did not slip us something on the sly.' She laughed, remembering that — sweets, sly.

Papa said, 'We did not have electricity when we were children. If we wanted to study, we were sent out to sit under the streetlight with our books. During the examinations, there would be a circle of students sitting and reciting their lessons aloud. It would be difficult to concentrate on law because others were reciting theorems or Sanskrit slokas or dates from British history. But we did it — we passed our exams.'

Papa said, 'The best student in my year studied day and night, day and night. We found out how he could study so much. During the exams, he cut off his eyelashes. Then, whenever his eyes shut, they would prick him and he would wake up so he could study more.'

Papa's stories tended to be painful. Mama's had to do with food — mostly sweets — and family. But the stories were few, and brief. That could have been tantalising — so much unsaid, left to be imagined — but the children did not give the past that

13

much thought because MamaPapa seemed sufficient in themselves. Having fused into one, they had gained so much in substance, in stature, in authority, that they loomed large enough as it was; they did not need separate histories and backgrounds to make them even more immense.

Sometimes one caught a glimpse of what they had been like before they were joined together in their Siamese twin existence on the veranda swing. At times Uma was astonished, even embarrassed by such a glimpse — for instance, of Mama playing a game of rummy with her friends which she did surreptitiously because Papa had a highminded disapproval of all forms of gambling. When Mama went across to the neighbours' for a morning game, she did not quite lift her sari to her knees and jump over the hedge but somehow gave the impression of doing so. Her manner — along with the curious patter that went with the game — became flirtatious, girlish. Her cheeks filled out plumply as she stuffed in the betel nuts and leaves she was offered — another indulgence frowned upon by Papa — her eyes gleamed with mischief as she tossed back her head and laughed apparently. without any thought of propriety. She clasped the cards to her chest and fluttered her lashes coquettishly. If Uma hung over her shoulders to look or Aruna edged closer to see why she seemed so delighted with her hand of cards, she swatted at her daughters as if they were a pair of troublesome flies. 'Go. Go play with your friends.'

Then she would come back to lunch, picking her way through a gap in the hedge, her daughters trailing after her, and by the time she arrived at the veranda, her manner had become the familiar one of guarded restraint, censure and a tired decorum.

When Papa, back from his office, asked what they had done with themselves all morning, she drooped, sighing, and fanned herself, saying, 'It was so-o hot, what can one do? Nothing.'

As for Papa, he never became less like himself, only more so. Calling for the driver to bring the car round in the morning, he got in with an air of urgency that suggested any delay could cause an explosion. If they ever had occasion to go to the office to fetch him, he would be sitting at an immense desk like the satrap of some small provinciality, mopping his neck with a large handkerchief, giving curt orders to his secretary, his typist and his clients, every gesture and grimace adding to the carapace of his authority till it

15

encased him in its dully glinting lead.

Mama would carefully pack his tennis kit and send it across to him with the office peon who had come for it on his bicycle. Pinning the bag under a metal clamp, he would pedal away. Mama would watch him turn out of the gate, onto the road, deep in thought.

Uma wondered if she pictured Papa changing into it in his office, behind the green oilcloth screen that stood across one corner. She put her fingers to her mouth to suppress a giggle.

Then Mama would sit herself down on the veranda swing, alone, to wait for him, keeping a cursory eye on the little girls as they played in the dry patch of grass where they were laying out a garden of pebbles, leaves, twigs and marigold petals. She intervened irritably when they quarrelled too loudly.

Afternoon dwindled to hazy evening and finally the car drove up. Papa jumped out and came up the steps to the veranda with a bound, swinging his racquet. He was dressed in the white cotton shorts Mama had sent him, their wide legs flapping about his thin shanks. The metal buckles had made rust marks at the waist. She often scolded the washerman for bringing back the shorts with rust marks from the wash.

She also scolded him for breaking the large white buttons that she then had to replace, spectacles on her nose, thin-lipped with concentration. Papa also wore a short-sleeved white shirt with a green or blue trim. He gleamed with effort and achievement and perspiration. 'Beat Shankar six–five, six–two,' he reported as he strode past them on his way to his dressing room, his cotton socks collapsing, exhausted, round his ankles. They heard him throw down his racquet with a pleased groan.

None of them spoke on the veranda. Mama sat as if stunned by his success, his prowess. Then they heard a bucket clanking, water sloshing. A stream of soapy water crept out of a drain in the side of the house and pushed past dry leaves and dust to end in a pool of slime under the basil and jasmine bushes. The girls stared.

Rousing herself, Mama called, 'Uma! Uma! Tell cook to bring Papa his lemonade!'

Uma ran.

There were social occasions of course — Papa's career required a large number of them — and some were witnessed by his children. At them, Papa was pleased to indulge himself in a little whisky and water.

When he had done so, he began to make what they considered rather frightening attempts at jocularity. His jokes were always directed against others, and they were quite ferocious under cover of the geniality that seemed proper to the ambience of a dinner party or a reception at the club. Having made some junior magistrate squirm uncomfortably with his sallies, or reminded a senior judge of an incident best forgotten and drawing only a sour twist of the lips in response, he himself would laugh heartily. The success of his joke was measured according to the amount of discomfort it caused others. It was his way of scoring, and he threw back his head and laughed in triumph, seemed physically to gain in stature (which was on the negligible side). One could be fooled into thinking Papa was in good spirits. But the family was not fooled: they knew he was actually rattled, shaken by what he saw as a possible challenge to his status. They were relieved when he returned to what was normal for him — taciturnity — with his authority unchallenged and unshaken.

One could be forgiven for thinking Papa's chosen role was scowling, Mama's scolding. Since every adult had to have a role, and these were their parents', the children did not question their choice. At least, not during their childhood.

Two

Papa has sent for the car. It takes the driver
a little time to change into his uniform,
more time to get it started and out of the garage (since Papa's retirement, the car and
driver, too, are semi-retired, rarely called
on). Papa stands on the veranda steps
watching its sagging, rusting body crawl
forwards with a grinding, reluctant groan.
He looks on impassively. When Uma says,
'That Rover is going to stop one day and
never start again — it's so *old*,' he remains
impassive, as if he prefers not to hear her
and has not heard her. And so the car, a
relic of Papa's past, arrives in the portico.
Papa gets into the front seat beside the
driver and waits for Mama and Uma to
climb into the back. He is taking them for
an outing to the park. He has spent all

Sunday pacing the veranda, now and then swinging his arms upwards, clasping his hands, or standing still and bending his knees as if in salute to the days when he played tennis, was young and vigorous. He has told the women they must get some exercise, they sit around the house too much. So they are being taken to the park.

As soon as they are at the park gates, which are very high and wide, of beautifully intricate wrought iron, now sagging, he jumps out and rushes in with great urgency. Unfortunately there are many other people in the park on a Sunday evening, sitting in groups and picnicking, or strolling around the beds of canna lilies and the waterless fountain. They are so many obstructions in his way — a child with a balloon or a mother with an infant pulling at her dress — and he is obliged to lower his head, square his shoulders and charge past them regardless.

Mama and Uma try to follow him but easily become distracted. They stop to look at a bush clipped to look like a peacock, at a jacaranda tree in bloom — its flowers a tender smoky blue on the bare branches — or pull away from a boisterous dog who has been rolling in the mud where a hosepipe is flooding the path and now

21

scatters muddy drops with abandon, then are brought up short by the spectacle of a shrivelled old man in a muslin dhoti so fine as to be diaphanous, who is absorbed in the yoga exercises he is performing with total concentration, as if utterly alone in that festive park. Mama pulls her sari tightly about her shoulders and says 'Tch, tch,' to express her distaste for such public display.

When they look up, they see Papa far ahead, striding along as if to keep an appointment. He does not stop to look at anyone, anything. Mama gives an annoyed little snort and tells Uma they will continue their walk by themselves and not try to keep up with Papa. Sedately, they circle the park, keeping to a path between the railing and the canna beds and pretending not to notice the peanut and icecream vendors thrusting their wares between the bars and calling to customers — Uma finds saliva gathering at the corners of her mouth at the smell of the spiced, roasted gram but decides to say nothing. Every now and then they catch sight of Papa: his blinding white shorts and his sombre energy make him stand out in the desultory, disorderly crowds. Then Mama's lashes flutter lightly in recognition. Admiration, too? Pride? Uma can never tell.

Just as they come to the end of their round, at the gate where the car and the driver are waiting, Papa arrives too. Magical timing. He of course has done three rounds in the time it has taken them to do one, but he refuses to look pleased. 'Get in,' he says impatiently, 'I've been waiting for you. So slow. So slow. Get in. Get in. Quick, now.'

Uma, scrambling in after Mama, says, 'Oof, Papa, why are we hurrying?'

Papa gives the driver orders all the way home. 'Turn here. Take this turning, not that one. Faster now — stop! Don't you see the bus in front of you? All right now, quick. Faster. Oof, so slow, so slow!'

'Why are we hurrying?' Uma asks again querulously.

Back home, Mama crumples into a listless heap of cotton. In a sinking voice, she breathes, 'Did you tell cook to have lemonade ready?'

Uma goes off to see to the lemonade and MamaPapa settle down on the swing, shuffle their feet out of their shoes and let them dangle, sigh, make a few adjustments and become two parts of one entity again, side by side, presenting the same indecipherable face to the world.

When visitors came and enquired after their health, one of them would reply in the first and sometimes third person singular, but the answer was made on behalf of both of them. If Papa gave his opinion of their local member of parliament or the chances of the government in the next election, Mama said nothing because he had spoken for her too. When Mama spoke of the sales at which she planned to buy towels or of the rise in the price of silver that made her wonder if it was time to sell her plate, Papa made assenting grunts because his thoughts were one with hers. Their opinion differed so rarely that if Mama refused to let Aruna wear a pearl necklace to the matinée at the Regal cinema or Papa decided Uma could not take music lessons after school, there was no point in appealing to the other parent for a different verdict: none was expected, or given.

Of course there were arguments between them, and debate. In fact, these occurred every day, at the same hour — when ordering meals for the day. This could never be done without heated discussion: that would have gone against custom. It was actually wonderful to see what fertile ground the dining table was for discussion and debate. But it was also impossible not to see that the verdict would be the same as at the outset — if Mama had suggested plain rice and mutton curry to begin with, then it would be that and no other, no matter what fancies had been entertained along the way: pilaos, kebabs, koftas . . . That was just part of the procedure.

The girls had learnt not to expect divergences and disagreements, and these occurred so rarely that they might not have recognised them when they did — if they had not been so acutely tuned to the temperature and the atmosphere of the house, so trained to catch the faintest inkling of any jarring, any dissonance.

And there had been, in that family, once, a major disagreement, one on the scale of a physical disaster, that left the family in a state of shock, as after a fire or flood. Mama, not Papa, administered that shock.

With Uma a grown woman — by some standards, at least — and Aruna newly discovering what it was to have periods, Mama it was who found herself pregnant.

It had taken the girls a long time to find out what was happening, what was the cause of so much whispering, furtive discussion, visits by the doctor and to the doctor. Older relatives were sent for, consultations were carried on. Mama's eyes were swollen with crying as she lay across her bed and wept. Papa scowled his concern and embarrassment. Like a blister with blood, the air was thick with secrets. The girls felt their ears creep as they strained to hear what was being said. It was incomprehensible, in some way risqué, even lewd, but they failed to understand the language although they caught the tone, and even the meaning. Something grossly physical — *sexual*. The word squealed loudly in their throats and they pressed their lips together so it should not escape. Uma had a vision of a frantic pig she had once seen in the bazaar, wriggling to escape from the butcher, and a memory of the whines and cries of mating dogs behind the servants' quarters, Papa's orders to the mali to drive them out with sticks. Aruna's vision was more domestic — petticoats and saris lifted, legs thrashing, *naked* legs, in the night, under the mosquito net. They'd heard sounds, muffled, escaping involuntarily from behind curtains. No doors were ever shut in that household: closed doors meant secrets, nasty secrets, impermissible. It meant authority would come stalking in and make a search to seize upon the nastiness, the unclean blot. Unclean, with human blood, woman's blood. But when it came to parents, one did not look. One looked down at oneself, ashamed. But still they strained to hear. Eventually, the servants told — ayah told them what might have been clear to anyone with eyes: it was a late pregnancy.

Mama was frantic to have it terminated. She had never been more ill, and would go through hellfire, she wept, just to stop the nausea that tormented her. But Papa set his jaws. They had two daughters, yes, quite grown-up as anyone could see, but there was no son. Would any man give up the chance of a son?

The pregnancy had to be accepted. Mama lay supine upon the bed, groaning through the summer from being overweight and sick. Above her the ceiling fan revolved with a repeated squeak and on the walls geckos clucked as they chased each other around. At her feet ayah, who had looked after Aruna when she was little and had to be called out of retirement in her village, sat massaging her legs with accompanying sounds of comfort and pacification. Uma and Aruna, alternately stricken by the atmosphere of the sickroom and titillated by expectation, hardly knew how that difficult summer unwound itself to the end. Then, when the monsoon came and the air became sticky and sweltering and mosquito-ridden and the geckos were scurrying around to snap up the flies, Mama was driven to Queen Mary's Hospital for Women and Children and there delivered of what she had suffered so much for — a son.

A son.

The whole family came to a standstill. Around Mama's bed, in the hospital, peering at this wonder. Even if Aruna did say, 'So red — so, *ugly!*' before she was nudged into silence, and Uma proved incapable of holding something so fragile and precious, they were acutely aware of the wonder of it. Mama's face, still tense from the difficult delivery, began to relax and broaden into long-suffering pride. It struck Uma later that from that hour onwards this became her habitual expression. But, to begin with, it was Papa who held their attention. In the hospital he seemed to be bottling up his emotions, to be holding them down with his formidable self-control. His face was quite contorted with the effort and perspiration broke out on his neck and soaked his shirt. He allowed himself to express his feelings only by uttering sharp orders to the nurses, to ayah, the girls, even supine Mama. Then he hurried his daughters away, almost before he had really looked at his son. In fact, he had looked away, as if that puny physical presence were irrelevant to the moment, and might even disappoint.

Arriving home, however, he sprang out of the car, raced into the house and shouted the news to whoever was there to hear. Servants, elderly relatives, all gathered at the door, and then saw the most astounding sight of their lives — Papa, in his elation, leaping over three chairs in the hall, one after the other, like a boy playing leap-frog, his arms flung up in the air and his hair flying. 'A boy!' he screamed, 'a bo-oy! Arun, Arun at last!' It turned out that when a second daughter had been born, the name Arun had already been chosen in anticipation of a son. It had had to be changed, in disappointment, to Aruna.

Uma and Aruna, in the portico, looking in, drew together, awe-struck.

Uma never overcame her awe of that extraordinary event, really far more memorable than the birth itself. As for Aruna, it could be said to have started a lifetime of bridling, of determined self-assertion.

When Mama came home, weak, exhausted and short-tempered, she tried to teach Uma the correct way of folding nappies, of preparing watered milk, of rocking the screaming infant to sleep when he was covered with prickly heat as with a burn. Uma, unfortunately, was her clumsy, undependable self, dropping and breaking things, frightenedly pulling away from her much too small, too precious, and too fragile brother.

'I have to go and do my homework,' she told her mother. 'I've got to get my sums done and then write the composition —'

'Leave all that,' Mama snapped at her.

Uma had received such directions from Mama before; Mama had never taken seriously the need to do any schoolwork, not having gone to school herself. 'We used to have a tutor, she said airily when the girls asked her how it was possible that she had not gone to school. 'He used to come to the house to teach us — a little singing — a little — hmm —' she became vague. 'We used to run away and hide from him,' she admitted, with a giggle. So Uma tried to explain that if she did not get her homework done, she would be sent to Mother Agnes with a note.

'But we are not sending you to Mother Agnes — or to school — again,' Mama said.

Uma's face, looking up from the stack of nappies she was trying to fold, seemed to irritate Mama. She twitched her toes and snapped 'We are not sending you back to school, Uma. You are staying at home to help with Arun.'

Uma turned around to look for explanation and support. In matters educational, Papa would surely support her. He was educated; it was he who sent her to the convent school in the first place.

Uma would have found it difficult to articulate where the appeal of the convent school lay. The visible details would have sounded banal: the strict rules of the morning assembly to which the girls were not admitted unless they had been examined at the door to see if their shoes were polished, their fingernails short and without paint, the ribbons on their hair white and not coloured; then the piano on which Sister Teresa banged out the hymns with such pounding certainty, such unvarying rhythm; the wonderfully still and composed figure of Mother Agnes, planted squarely on her feet in large sandals, holding the prayer book from which she read in her deep, unhurried voice that seemed to move between the girls like a slow brown river; the orderliness of her office room to which Uma was fairly frequently sent with a note from the teacher,

and where she looked around avidly, at the
picture on the wall of a golden-haired Jesus
holding a lamb, the tinted print over the
mantelpiece of the tear-stained face of a
child gazing up at a corner of the gilt frame
where a silver star shone, or the polished
brass vase with its spray of stiff fresh flowers
on the desk and the clean white linen run-
ners on top of the bookshelf, the immense
clock near the door immensely ticking, and
the view from the window of a garden of
marvellous tidiness, the long verandas en-
closing a courtyard that they could look on
but not jump into because the grass was so
precious and the roses so rare . . .

She would probably have listed the
games they played hectically on the
playing fields to the sharp blasts of a
whistle blown by Miss D' Souza; the spot-
less condition of the sickroom where there
was certain to be a remedy for every headache, every bruise and cut; the new copy-
books with lined pages and the crisp inky
textbooks they were handed out at the beginning of term along with a new wooden
ruler and a clean eraser; the sayings and
proverbs the nuns employed in their
speech that sounded so wise, so indisput-
able ('It's no use crying over spilt milk'
and 'A stitch in time saves nine'); the cele-

bration of Christmas and of Easter and the saints' days.

She would have confessed how the order pleased her, the rationality of the whole system, each element having its own function and existing for a reason. She would have explained how it satisfied her that every question was answered, every doubt dealt with. As an infant she had sung louder than any other child in class:

'Jesus loves me; this I know,
For the Bible tells me so!'

She knew that something secret went on in the small chapel where the children were not allowed, where one could only catch a glimpse, occasionally, of a nun in prayer, kneeling before an altar where a streak of gilt showed in the shadows; she knew it was in some manner linked to the subterranean feelings stirred within her by the words intoned during prayers:

'The Lord is my shepherd;
   I shall not want.
He maketh me to lie down
   in green pastures:
He leadeth me beside the still waters.
He restoreth my soul. . . .'

Clearly, the outer plainness and regularity of this convent world contained within it secret chambers dark with mystery, streaked with golden promise.

So she could not understand when others, like Aruna, cursed it and loathed it with such bitterness. Why? Uma was at school before any other child, and every day she searched for an excuse to stay on. School was not open long enough. There were the wretched weekends when she was plucked back into the trivialities of her home, which seemed a denial, a negation of life as it ought to be, sombre and splendid, and then the endless summer vacation when the heat reduced even that pointless existence to further vacuity. She prickled with impatience for the fifteenth of July when school would re-open and a new term begin. She hurried to buy the new books, gloated over their freshness, wrapped them in brown paper covers to keep them clean, eager for the day when they would be put to use.

True, there was one uncomfortable fact that could not be denied: in spite of her raging enthusiasm, she was an abject scholar. Why? It was so unfair. The nuns clucked and shook their heads and sent for Mama, wrote notes to Papa, and every year, after the exams, said sorrowfully that they would have to hold her back — she had managed to fail every single test: in English, Hindi, history, geography, arithmetic, drawing, and even domestic science! There was not a thing Uma put her hand to that did not turn to failure. Uma rubbed and rubbed at her exercise books with an increasingly black and stumpy eraser, struggled to work out her sums, to remember dates, to spell 'Constantinople'; and over and over again she failed. Her record book was marked red for failure. The other girls, their own books marked healthily in green and blue for success and approval, looked at her with pity on the day the record book was handed out. She wept with shame and frustration.

So now Mama was able to say, 'You know you failed your exams again. You're not being moved up. What's the use of going back to school? Stay at home and look after your baby brother.' Then, seeing Uma's hands shake as she tried to continue with folding the nappies, she seemed to feel a little pity. 'What is the use of going back to school if you keep failing, Uma?' she asked in a reasonable tone. 'You will be happier at home. You won't need to do any lessons. You are a big girl now. We are trying to arrange a marriage for you. Not now,' she added, seeing the panic on Uma's face. 'But soon. Till then, you can help me look after Arun. And learn to run the house.' She reached out her hand to catch Uma's. 'I need your help, beti,' she coaxed, her voice sweet with pleading.

Uma wrenched her hand free.

Three

'Uma, pass your father the fruit.'

Uma picks up the fruit bowl with both hands and puts it down with a thump before her father. Bananas, oranges, apples — there they are, for him.

Blinking, he ignores them. Folding his hands on the table, he gazes over them with the sphinx-like expression of the blind.

Mama knows what is wrong. She taps Uma on the elbow. 'Orange,' she instructs her. Uma can no longer pretend to be ignorant of Papa's needs, Papa's ways. After all, she has been serving them for some twenty years. She picks out the largest orange in the bowl and hands it to Mama who peels it in strips, then divides it into separate segments. Each segment is then peeled and freed of pips and threads till only the perfect globules of juice are left, and then passed, one by one, to the edge of Papa's plate. One by one, he lifts them with the tips of his fingers and places them in his mouth. Everyone waits while he repeats the gesture, over and over. Mama's lips are pursed with the care she gives her actions, and their importance.

When she has done, and only pith and peel and pips lie on her plate, and nothing at all on Papa's except for the merest smear of juice, she glances over at Uma. Her dark eyes flash with the brightness of her achievement and pride.

'Where is Papa's finger bowl?' she asks loudly.

The finger bowl is placed before Papa. He dips his fingertips in and wipes them on the napkin. He is the only one in the family who is given a napkin and a finger bowl; they are emblems of his status.

Mama sits back. The ceremony is over. She has performed it. Everyone is satisfied.

☙

It was that time of day when the cook had closed up his kitchen and gone off to his quarters behind the guava trees to stretch out on his string bed and sleep till teatime,

Mama and the baby were both silent in the dark, shuttered bedroom, and the girls left to themselves under the revolving fan, on the stripped-down beds of the room they shared, for the time being, with Mama's elderly cousin who was still around to help. The elderly cousin was beyond the need for sleep — she thought it an indulgence of the young — and coaxed the girls into playing a game of cards. They sat cross-legged on the bed, slapping down the cards in a desultory way, now and then letting out an exclamation of disgust or triumph and leaning forward to gather up their gains.

Uma muttered, 'I'm going to get a drink of water — I'll come back —' and slipped out of the door. Aruna watched her sharply because she had seen that Uma's mind was not on the cards. But Uma was prepared for the afternoon — in spite of the distress that had made her throat dry and her hands shake, she had planned carefully. Now she went quietly to that corner of the pantry where, behind a tall stack of dinner plates, she had hidden her purse containing all the money she had, in a tight roll. Soundlessly she slipped into the sandals she had left behind the water jar on the veranda outside the kitchen, dropped down off the parapet and darted into the shade of the guava trees.

She knew all the rooms in the house had their curtains drawn against the midday sun, all the verandas their reed mats unrolled and hanging down in the dull yellow air. She counted on the servants' families, scattered about the compound, being heavily asleep. True, a koel was calling in the neem tree — piercingly, questingly, over and over again — but its voice was the voice of summer itself; noticeable when it first arrived, along with the blaze and the lethargy of the season, and then just a part of the background, a thread in its worn, faded fabric.

Keeping close to the hedge, she held her head down and darted along. The mali lived in a hut close to the gate, but had screened himself so heavily with vines and bushes and hedges, he hardly even noticed the comings and goings along the drive unless specifically asked to do so. As she hoped, he was lying on his string cot by his hibiscus bush where the tap dripped pleasantly into a pool of mud whereby he kept himself cool. He was asleep with his mouth open, his breath coming and going in a tuneless song. Uma was uncharacteristically quiet this afternoon, making her sandals shuffle through, not slap at the gravel.

Then she went out of the gate with a

sudden whisk and broke into a run. Clutching her purse to her — a tiny yellow plastic one the elderly cousin had brought her as a present — she ran along the ridge of heaped earth and garbage between the road and the ditch. Uma was always unsteady on her feet — much as she loved the games played at school, she was inept at all of them — and the ridge was uneven, so she hobbled and stumbled in a way that would have made any passerby nervous to see. Only there was no passerby at that time of day, not in their part of town which had little traffic at any time. She ran all the way to the crossing where she knew rickshaws waited for custom, and she was right: there were three drawn up in the shade of a large rain tree. Their drivers lay across the benches, asleep, legs hanging over the sides, but Uma made such a din, crying, 'Take me to St Mary's School, to St Mary's School, quick,' that one of them stirred, sat up, adjusted his red and white checked turban and with a twitch of his mouth indicated that she should get in. Then he panted and huffed so hugely as he pedalled down the road in the midday blaze that Uma feared he would collapse with heat stroke. Then she would not get to St Mary's and Mother Agnes. And she would not —

Hrr, hrr, hrr, the rickshaw driver's lungs and legs pumped, and the dust flared up from the road into their faces and eyes, stinging. So, out of breath and cloaked in dust, they arrived at St Mary's. After paying him off — he loudly demanded more, then more still, and finally bullied her into handing over all she had — she stood at the gate and realised that it was the hour for the nuns to rest as well as everyone else, and that Mother Agnes ought not to be disturbed. She had never dared disturb Mother Agnes before.

Yet, knowing that, she still dared. There was no alternative. Flying down the stone corridors, she ran past classrooms shut for the summer, up the stairs to the nuns' private quarters where the schoolgirls never went, were not permitted. All the doors leading off the verandas here were shut as well. In addition, their glass panes were curtained. How was she to tell which was Mother's? The curtains were the same blue cotton at every door. Unlike the classroom doors, their panes were polished and the brass handles shone. There were pots of ferns beside them, and doormats outside them. But no sign of anyone.

Then Mother Agnes came round the corner and down the passage, walking in long, rustling strides towards her. Uma did not know why she should be out at this time, what she might be doing. Certainly she could not have been looking for Uma, and yet that was what she seemed to be doing, her face emerging from her coif, her voice calling, 'Child?'

Uma hurled herself at Mother Agnes, threw her arms around her waist, hid her face in the starched white cotton skirts, and howled aloud. She was a messy weeper: her face was wet, her hair distraught. Her mouth was twisted and her eyes and nose ran. She knotted her hands in Mother's skirts and girdle. All the time she howled. 'Mother, oh Mother,' she wailed, and when Mother Agnes tried to pluck her off her skirts and hold her aside, she flung herself down at the nun's sandalled feet and lay on the floor, abjectly wailing.

'Uma!' the nun recognised her at last — and seemed quite resigned to dealing with yet another child who had failed her exams and come to plead for promotion. 'Will you get up, please? Come into my room, please. This is no way, you know, child —' and she bent and pulled Uma to her feet, then took her face and pressed it to her bosom. Uma, startled, breathed in the smell of antiseptic soap and starch and a whiff of something else — some kind of scent, musky, *religious* — while Mother Agnes muttered a prayer (it sounded like a prayer) into her hair.

But when she heard why Uma had run to her, what Uma wished her to do, she tapped a brass paperknife on the edge of the desk and her eyes became hooded while her face receded into her coif. 'Hmm, hmm,' she said, listening to Uma's sobs. 'Yes, your father wrote to me — I know. He says that because you have failed once again —'

Uma let out another howl because she had forgotten about that failure and only now remembered. 'But I will work very hard!' she yelled. 'I will pass next time. Please tell him, Mother — I *will* pass next time!'

The more she yelled, the more dubious Mother looked. When Uma gabbled about the baby, not knowing how to bathe the baby, about being afraid to pin on his nappy, she began to grow impatient. 'Girls have to learn these things too, you know,' she said.

Uma was thunderstruck. It was the last thing she ever expected Mother Agnes to say. Now Mother Agnes was talking about the Virgin Mary and baby Jesus — but surely she did not think the Virgin Mary was a mother like Mama was a mother? Surely she did not think baby Jesus ever lay squalling in his crib with his hair growing down his forehead and over his ears, with dribble running out of the corner of his mouth like a sick cat? That he had to have his nappies changed and that they smelt? Uma stared at Mother Agnes in dismay. It *was* what Mother was saying. And if she wound up by giving Uma a holy picture out of the drawer in her desk — a small, gilt-edged card with a waxily pink Jesus on a waxily white Virgin Mary's blue lap, and advising her to pray for strength, pray to the Virgin Mary for strength, never forget to pray, she was nevertheless dismissing her, not only from her presence, her protection, but even from her school.

She got to her feet, drawing Uma up too. But as she held Uma by her shoulders, trying to convey her own belief and her strength to her, Uma suddenly went limp and crumpled and the next thing that Mother Agnes knew was that Uma was lying stretched out on the cotton rug by her desk. Nor had she simply fainted — she was writhing, frothing a little at the mouth and moaning, banging her head to one side, then the other. When Mother Agnes tried to lift her, she began to roll so violently that Mother Agnes had to go to the door and call for help.

Then the ignominy of her return, in the school van, accompanied by Sister Teresa and the school nurse, with Aruna wide-eyed and Mama scolding like a madwoman, blaming it all on the pink and blue and gilt picture that Mother Agnes had given Uma and that she still held clenched in her fist. The way Mama railed against it, it would seem the holy picture was a poison potion, or some evil charm that had cast a spell on her daughter. 'See what these nuns do,' she raged to Papa. 'What ideas they fill in the girls' heads! I always said don't send them to a convent school. Keep them at home, I said — but who listened? And now — !'

When Mama was calm again, she showed Uma how to pour a little oil on her finger-tips and then massage it into the baby's limbs. Massaging made him ticklish; he wriggled and writhed under her fingers like a fish trying to escape, and after biting her lips in an attempt not to, Uma did burst out laughing after all.

Mama turned away with a sigh of relief: clearly she felt all was well now — the baby could be left to his elder sister.

'But ayah can do this — ayah can do

that —' Uma tried to protest when the orders began to come thick and fast. This made Mama look stern again. 'You know we can't leave the baby to the servant,' she said severely. 'He needs proper attention.' When Uma pointed out that ayah had looked after her and Aruna as babies, Mama's expression made it clear it was quite a different matter now, and she repeated threateningly: 'Proper attention.'

Proper attention. It was with a steely determination that Mama turned this upon her son as if making sure no one could accuse her of any lapse in his care or recall the reluctance with which she had borne him. Even when she turned him over to Uma, or the ayah, to be bathed or dressed, she remained sharply vigilant of their performance. As for his meals, she watched over him like a dragon, determined that a fixed quantity of milk was poured down his gullet whether he wanted it or not and, later, the prescribed boiled egg and meat broth. Then, when Papa returned from the office, he would demand to know how much his son had consumed and an answer had to be given: it had to be precise and it had to be one that pleased.

For Arun's birth did not mean that

MamaPapa were finally separated into two entities — Mama Papa — not at all: Arun appeared to be the glue that held them together even more inextricably. If Mama managed to have a little private life of her own — those games of rummy, those secret betel leaves, 'female' talk with her daughters when the occasion arose — then, where Arun was concerned, she and Papa became one again. He would ask the questions about his son's rearing and care, she would supply the answers: all her duties and responsibilities neatly accounted for like so many laundered sheets back from the wash.

More than ever now, she was Papa's helpmeet, his consort. He had not only made her his wife, he had made her the mother of his son. What honour, what status. Mama's chin lifted a little into the air, she looked around her to make sure everyone saw and noticed. She might have been wearing a medal.

It was not that their lives changed in more than a few details such as their shared concern for their son. No, their social life did not miss a beat; Mama continued to deck herself in silks and jewellery and accompany Papa to the club, to dinner parties and weddings. After all, Uma and Aruna and the ayah were there to stand in for her at Arun's cot. It seemed to them that Mama sailed out with an added air of achievement. She had matched Papa's achievement, you could say, and they were now more equal than ever.

Was *this* love? Uma wondered disgustedly, was *this* romance? Then she sighed, knowing such concepts had never occurred to Mama: she did not read, and she did not go to the cinema. When her friends or neighbours gossiped about a 'love marriage' they had heard of, she lifted her upper lip a little bit, to convey her scorn. Love marriage indeed, *she* knew better.

Uma also noticed how Mama and Papa looked upon Arun with an identical expression: a kind of nervous, questioning, somewhat doubtful but determined pride. He was their son, surely an object of pride. Surely? Then, seeing this puny creature who appeared to take forever to raise his head, or get to his knees, finally to stand upon his legs, a kind of secret doubt would enter their eyes, even a panic — quickly suppressed, quickly brushed away.

Mama developed a nervous fear on the subject of Arun's feeding: the exercise always left her spent, and after it she still had to face Papa's interrogation regarding its success or failure. Arun seemed to become infected by her nervousness, the tension surrounding the whole occasion. As soon as the boiled egg in a cup or the bowl of broth appeared, he clenched his teeth and turned away, pretending to be engrossed in play from which no one could distract him. They took it in turns to try — Mama, Uma and the ayah — to spoon mouthfuls into him when he was not looking. Occasionally they managed to catch him unawares so that he would swallow before he knew it, but mostly he averted his face at just the right moment, or else spat out what they had forced in. Mama was often in tears by the end of it, and Uma in a raging temper, while Papa would say, 'And have you seen the Joshis' son? He is already playing cricket!'

It was years before they understood what Arun's tastes were, and accepted the fact that he would not touch the meat Papa insisted he should eat: Arun was a Vegetarian.

Papa was confounded. A meat diet had been one of the revolutionary changes brought about in his life, and his brother's, by their education. Raised amongst traditional vegetarians, their eyes had been opened to the benefits of meat along with that of cricket and the English language: the three were linked inextricably in their minds. They had even succeeded in convincing the wives they married of this novel concept of progress, and passed it on to their children. Papa was always scornful of those of their relatives who came to visit and insisted on clinging to their cereal- and vegetable-eating ways, shying away from the meat dishes Papa insisted on having cooked for dinner.

Now his own son, his one son, displayed this completely baffling desire to return to the ways of his forefathers, meek and puny men who had got nowhere in life. Papa was deeply vexed. He prescribed cod liver oil. Mama and Uma were to spoon it down his throat. Somehow. Holding his nose pinched between her fingers, Uma was to force it between his teeth. He did open his mouth — but snapped his teeth shut on her finger. Withdrawing it with a yell, she stared at the blood trickling down. 'Did you *see?*' she gasped. 'Did you see what he *did?*'

'You remember, you bit me once?' she reminded him, holding a quarter of green guava just out of his reach.

They were hiding in a clump of bougain-villaeas, she with the guava she had picked unripe and cut into quarters and eighths and sprinkled with salt for a treat.

A strongly forbidden treat. Suffering as he

did from an endless procession of ills — he had already run through mumps, measles, chicken pox, bronchitis, malaria, 'flu, asthma, nosebleeds and more — it was the last thing Arun ought to have been given as a treat: fruit so unripe that it set the teeth on edge and turned the gullet sore. Yet she was pushing the slices into his mouth, and her own, wickedly irresponsible. They closed their eyes and winced as the tartness rasped the tastebuds at the roots of their tongues. Even their ears crept, the fruit was so sour. They blinked their eyes shut and tears pricked the corners with salt. They opened them and laughed.

'See my finger? See where you bit me?' Uma waved it under his nose, not wanting him to forget because she had not forgotten.

Arun narrowed his eyes in a way that made Uma shift uncomfortably on her haunches: she ought not to have expected Arun to enjoy the joke.

'Shall I tell MamaPapa what you gave me to eat?' he retaliated craftily. 'What will MamaPapa do if they know what you gave me to eat?'

Uma jumped up so quickly that her hair caught in the thorny bougainvillaeas and lifted it off her head so that she seemed to be hanging by it. Arun screamed with laughter.

Four

Mama and Papa are at a wedding reception to which Uma has refused to go: now that Papa is retired, there are so few occasions when they leave the house, Uma has grown to prize them. She has eaten her supper on a tray; she has looked through her card and her bangle collection. Hearing someone move about in the other room, she has quickly put these out of sight. But it is only ayah. Ayah has brought in some laundry from the washerman and come to put it away. She brings in an armful of petticoats for Uma. Uma picks up her brush and starts brushing her hair to show ayah she is getting ready for bed.

'Come, Baby, I will do it for you,' ayah offers.

Uma begins to refuse with annoyance —

she does not particularly want ayah around, she had thought she was alone in the house — but when ayah takes the brush from her, she surrenders it. Sitting down, with ayah rhythmically slapping at her head with the brush, she feels about six years old.

Ayah came to them when Uma was three years old and Aruna was born. Retired, she returned to help with Arun when Mama was so distraught over his birth, and stayed on after he outgrew her and left home. Mama has grown used to having her around and likes having her do little things around the house — 'top work' she calls it, although Papa thinks these could be done by Uma, at a saving. Ayah knows she had better show him she earns her keep; whenever anyone looks her way, she instantly finds something to do. Mama has to keep up the pretence, too, and can always think up something. 'Go and see if the washerman has our things ready,' she will say, or, 'Tell cook to cut up some mangoes for tea.' When she can think of absolutely nothing else, she will lie back with a little sigh; then ayab edges forward, knowing this is a sign she wants her feet pressed, and she squats down and begins to knead and massage the feet Mama does not exactly proffer — in fact, she makes an irritated sound of refusal, but not strongly

54

enough to be meant.

Uma does not care for such physical attention. She pulls her head away: it is beginning to feel battered. 'Where's Lakshmi?' she asks, about the daughter who is a perennial source of drama.

'Oh, Baby, don't ask about that Lakshmi,' ayah sighs, and the hand that wields the brush comes to a stop, heavily. 'That wretch, she will see me dead soon. Trouble, trouble — what else to expect from Lakshmi? The day she was born was a cursed day.'

'Why? What's happened now?' Uma murmurs, reluctantly agreeing to listen to another tale.

'Oh, Baby, why ask? Do you want to hear what she has done now? Left that husband I managed to get for her, and run off. To find herself work, she says. What work is she to find, eh, tell me? Is she willing to lift even a finger to work? But she thinks she can get a job in some house and they will feed her and clothe her. As if having a job means becoming the daughter of the house.' Ayah sighs sadly. 'I have told her beatings are what she will get —'

'Why? Why do you say that? Maybe she'll find a good home to work in.'

'What good home will take *her?*' ayah

snaps back. 'One look at her is enough to tell you what *she* is good for! The other day, I asked her, where'd you get that bangle that you're jingling in my ears, eh? Just tell me where it comes from! I beat her and beat her till blood ran from her nose, but did she tell me? Not that one, curse of my life —'

'Why do you beat her?' Uma snatches her brush away from ayah. 'You are always beating that poor girl.'

'You think *she* is poor — not I, her mother, who has suffered all these years, spent good money on her wedding, gone without food and clothing to raise her —'

'No, you haven't. You get food in our kitchen and Mama gives you clothes. You are very well dressed.'

Ayah stares at her, scandalised, holding out her ripped and faded sari. 'You call these clothes? I call it a shame. It is an immodesty to dress in these rags. But what can I do? I must take what I can get. We are not all born fortunate —' and here she strikes the heel of her palm against her forehead and groans.

Uma gets up, annoyed. She has fallen into ayah's trap again. She marches up to her cupboard and flings it open. 'Oh, all right, take my saris off me. Ask, ask, till you have all I can give. Then you may be satisfied —'

and she pulls out two or three cotton saris and flings them at ayah with a show of temper she has learnt from Mama. With a quick afterthought, she snatches back one that is almost new and that she particularly likes — a pretty marigold yellow with a purple border — and shoves it out of sight at the back of the shelf.

Ayah is all smiles and beams. She picks them off the floor and clutches them to her, then vanishes from the room before her good fortune runs out. Uma bangs the cupboard door shut and locks it fiercely: her evening is spoilt.

∽

At regular intervals through the years, a yellow postcard would arrive from Mira-masi to say she would be stopping with them on her way from one pilgrimage place to another. Uma would invariably cry out 'Mira-masi? Oh, I love Mira-masi — she makes the very best ladoos. Mm, so round and big and sweet!' Mama was always incensed, a slur having been cast on the ladoos made in her kitchen. 'What a greedy child you are, Uma! I'm not going to let Mira-masi into the kitchen. She turns everything upside down and demands a new set of cooking pots, as if ours are unclean. And she won't eat what the cook makes — she is so old-fashioned.' Mama looked thoroughly put out.

Mira-masi was not her sister but a very distant relative, the second or possibly even the third wife of a relative Mama preferred not to acknowledge at all. He, fortunately, had been content to live in obscurity till — eventually, conveniently — he died, but this wife of his had in her widowhood developed an unsettling habit of travelling all over the country, quite alone, safe in her widow's white garments, visiting one place of pilgrimage after another like an obsessed tourist of the spirit, and only too often her hapless relatives by marriage found themselves in her way, at convenient stopping places. 'She never writes to ask if she may come,' Mama fumed, 'only to say that she *is* coming.' Since Mama generally enjoyed visitors, especially relatives with whom she could gossip about all the branches of the family and who put her in touch with them so that she did not feel so sorry for herself for being the one who lived far from them all, exiled by Papa and his career, Uma wondered why Mira-masi was the exception.

Uma would have thought that she would be the most welcome of all since Mira-masi was constantly visiting relatives, even the most remotely situated, and brought news of them — births, marriages, deaths, illnesses, scandals, litigation, gossip, rumours, prattle, tittle-tattle. . . . If only that were all she brought, Mama's groan seemed to imply. Unfortunately, gossip was just one aspect of Mira-masi's life — the social one — but there were others that were distinctly antisocial.

Ever since her widowhood, she had taken up religion as her vocation. Her day was ruled by ritual, from the moment she woke to make her salutations to the sun, through her ritual bath and morning prayers, to the preparation of her widow's single and vegetarian meal of the day (that Arun found so appetising that he wolfed it down in a way Mama took as an affront), and through the evening ceremonies at the temples she visited. Only at night, after spreading out on the floor the rush mat that she brought with her, would she sit down crosslegged and relate to Mama all the annals of the family (Mama was avid to hear the gossip yet bristled to think Mira-masi could consider it *her* family when she was only the second, possibly the third wife of an unspeakable member of it, so her listening face was contorted with all her battling emotions and was a sight worth seeing). Then, when

Mama had been called away by an increasingly irate Papa who did not tolerate his wife's attention straying from him and was being kept awake by their voices besides, it would be Uma's turn. Curling up on the mat, around Mira-masi's comfortable lap, one hand on her thumping, wagging knee, Uma would listen to her relate those ancient myths of Hinduism that she made sound as alive and vivid as the latest gossip about the family. To Mira-masi the gods and goddesses she spoke of, whose tales she told, were her family, no matter what Mama might think — Uma could see that.

She never tired of hearing the stories of the games and tricks Lord Krishna played as a child and a cowherd on the banks of the Jumna, or of the poet-saint Mira who was married to a raja and refused to consider him her husband because she believed she was already married to Lord Krishna and wandered through the land singing songs in his praise and was considered a madwoman till the raja himself acknowledged her piety and became her devotee. Best of all was the story of Raja Harishchandra who gave up his wealth, his kingdom and even his wife to prove his devotion to the god Indra and was reduced to the state of tending cremation fires for a living; his own wife was brought to him for her cremation when at last the god took pity on him and restored her to life. Then Uma, with her ears and even her finger-tips tingling, felt that here was someone who could pierce through the dreary outer world to an inner world, tantalising in its colour and romance. If only it could *replace* this, Uma thought hungrily.

It was her passion to attempt this miracle that made her follow Mira-masi through the cycle of the day's rituals, even crouch beside her at the outdoor hearth specially built for her with bricks and clay so that she could cook her own meals at a safe distance from the cook who laughed contemptuously in the kitchen where he fried up onions and garlic and stirred the mutton curries and grilled the kebabs that made Mira-masi cover her mouth and nose with the loose end of her sari and choke. Uma was not allowed to touch anything. 'Did you bathe when you came home from school? No? Did you bathe after going to the toilet? *No?* Do you have your period now? Don't touch, child, don't touch!' But Uma would only shift a few inches away, still hugging her knees and watching Mira-masi chop up the greens that were all she would eat. Sometimes she was allowed to bring out flour and milk and sugar to her so she could make

61

sweets for the family — those famous ladoos.

Mira-masi would take her along on her evening visit to the temple for the puja. They would walk down the road together and turn into the lane at the end of which stood a pink stucco temple lit with blue fluorescent tubes and hung with oleographs of Mira-masi's chosen deity, Shiva. Here Uma would be overcome with shyness and hang back at the door, preferring to watch Mira-masi march through, giving the brass bell overhead a mighty clang before going up to the shrine where she mingled with the throng of devotees, all reaching out for drops of holy water dribbled into their cupped hands by the priest with his tray full of red powder and yellow marigolds. Then all the bells would ring — tang! tang! — and the conch-shells blow — hrr-oom, hrr-oom — and the priest would circle a trayful of lamps around the god's head, reciting verses in somewhat nasal Sanskrit, and finally come out to distribute sweets to the faithful. Then Uma would quickly hide behind a pillar. Mira-masi went through these rituals as casually as if she were dusting her house: one would not have thought it was the central activity of her life. It was Uma who failed to take them casually: they assaulted her very being and made her shake like the pennant flying over the temple gate.

She found it easier to participate in the private arrangements for worship that Mira-masi created whenever she came to stay. An altar would be made by setting out on a shelf, or a low table, or even on a few bricks placed together, the objects that accompanied her when she travelled: a little brass Shiva (she called it golden), an oil lamp, an oleograph, and a copy of the Ramayana wrapped in red cotton. Immediately on waking, Uma would go into the garden — and the dew on the dusty grass would transfer itself to her bare feet and the hem of her nightie — and tug a few roses and marigolds off their stems, or collect a handful of white jasmine that had bloomed in the night and lay scattered beneath the bush at dawn, resolutely ignoring the angry shouts of the mali. Hurrying back to Mira-masi's room, she would place them at the altar, grateful and amazed that she was allowed to perform so important a ceremony with her polluted hands. Mira-masi would seat herself before her home-made altar, her eyes closed as she recited the Lord's names over and over in a fervent manner that made her sway as if she were possessed. In these moments there was graven on her face, as on a stone image, an expression so fervent that it awed Uma. If her eyes opened, they flashed with fervour, almost ferociously. Then she would burst into song and in a ringing voice sing:

'I have travelled over the earth,
I have searched the whole earth,
Now at the lotus feet of the Lord,
I have found my salvation . . .'

and Uma felt she had been admitted to some sanctuary that had been previously closed to her. The nuns at St Mary's had allowed her as far as its portals — the assembly room, the hymn-singing — but she had never been admitted into their chapel, and that was where she had wanted to go, sensing this was the heart of their celebration. Now Mira-masi included her in the celebration, she was counted in, a member, although of what, she could not say.

The best part of Mira-masi's visit would be the obligatory trip to the river that Mama and Papa themselves did not permit their children, saying it was too hot, too dangerous, too dusty, too diseased, too crowded — in every way inadvisable. But they could not refuse Mira-masi what was to her a taste of paradise, and allowed her, rather grimly, to take the children when she went for her ritual dip, first taking them aside to warn them not to go near the water, keep well away from the river's edge and keep a watch out for crocodiles and death by drowning.

The warning proved unnecessary for both Arun and Aruna who went no further than the top of the stone steps leading down to the river, looking down at its sluggish flow and the line of washermen and pilgrims and boatmen with disdain; neither of them would have considered putting a foot into it, or a toe: they were too mindful of their health and safety.

Only Uma tucked her frock up into her knickers and waded in with such thoughtless abandon that the pilgrims, the washermen, the priests and boatmen all shouted, 'Watch out! Take care, child!' and pulled Uma back before she sank up to her chin and the current carried her away. It had not occurred to her that she needed to know how to swim, she had been certain the river would sustain her.

Mira-masi had been too immersed in her devotions to notice. Knee-deep in water, she was pouring water over herself, chanting the Lord's name in ringing triumph, oblivious that a boatman nearby had grasped Uma by her hair and pulled her to safety onto the sandy bank where she lay gasping and flopping and trickling like a grounded fish. Mira-masi was too gloriously preoccupied to pay attention but Arun and Aruna could hardly wait to get home and report to their parents Uma's ridiculous and crazy behaviour for which both she and Mira-masi were severely reprimanded.

An idea grew within the family that Uma and Mira-masi were partners in mischief.

Five

A bicycle rickshaw turns in at the gate and its
bell gives an announcing ring; it has a
cracked sound — t-rring, t-rring. The family
on the veranda lowers its papers, sewing, fans
and fly swatters, and stares: no one was expected. But it stops in the portico and a
dishevelled figure climbs out awkwardly and
throws a bag onto the steps before paying off
the rickshaw driver who stands astraddle his
bicycle, mopping his neck with his headcloth.

Mama and Papa squint their little eyes,
suspicious and incredulous. Uma goes to
the edge of the terrace to explore. Suddenly
she shrieks, 'Oh, Ramu-bhai! It is Ramu-
bhai!' and goes hurrying down the steps so
fast that her slippers strike at her heels —
slap, slap, slap.

Ramu turns around and grins at her. His

eyebrows and hair are clay-coloured with dust; his khaki clothes are blackened with soot. Picking up his bag, he gives it a cheerful swing and asks cockily, 'Any room at the inn? Can you have me?'

'Come, come,' Uma cries. 'Come up here. Mama, Papa, look who has come!'

Mama and Papa are looking, but with such pinched expressions, such tight-lipped disapproval, that it is clear they do not share Uma's delight in seeing the black sheep of the family who has the bad manners to turn up without notice. Both the parents draw their feet together as if to avoid a gutter that runs too close.

But Ramu beams at them as if he does not recognise the signs of a cold welcome, or is entirely used to them and accepting of them. He has a club foot and wears an orthopaedic boot to steady him so he clomps across the terrace towards them. The bag weighs him down at one arm so his progress is slow. Uma rushes to take it from him.

'No, no,' he says, slapping her hand away. 'Ladies cannot carry bags for gents.'

She titters with pleasure: ladies! gents! 'Shall I get some tea?' she asks eagerly.

'We have just finished tea,' Mama says, unsticking her lips with some difficulty. 'You will have to order more.'

'I will get it,' Uma volunteers cheerfully, and lifts the teapot by its handle, swinging it so that she nearly knocks the spout off against the swing.

'Be *careful*, Uma,' Mama snaps.

When she leaves, there is silence for a bit because both parents seem to have decided to use silence as a weapon against an unwelcome guest and insufficiently respectful nephew. In that silence, Ramu lowers himself into a creaking basket chair and spreads out his legs and throws back his head. A mynah on the neem tree that overhangs the terrace is watching his movements and lets out a series of whistles as if in comment upon them. Ramu-bhai returns a whistle to it.

'Thirty-six hours on the train — third class,' he tells them. 'I feel I'm made of soot.' He slaps at his thighs and shoulders to show them what he means. Then he stamps his orthopaedic boot and more dust flies. The mynah takes off with a squawk of alarm.

Mama looks as if she would like to do so too. Her lips have narrowed till they almost disappear into her chin. 'And where are you coming from?' she asks. 'Bombay?'

'Oh *no*, I have been travelling all over. I went to Trivandrum with a friend. His guru lives there and was having a birthday celebration at his ashram, but the food was so *awful,* I left him to it and went on my own to Cochin. It was much better — a port, sailors coming off the boats, everyone having a whale of a time. Then I took the boat to Goa where I ran into —'

'You need a bath,' Mama interrupts.

'Oh, I need a long, hot bath. In good time. But first tea, please, tea!'

Uma is hurrying back with a refilled pot. She is humming. 'I've told cook to heat some bath water,' she cries, 'and he is going to make puris for breakfast.'

'Puris for breakfast?' Papa exclaims, breaking his silence. 'Puris? Puris? Did you say puris?' The words explode from him with both excitement and horror: it is what they have on special occasions. Uma must be out of her mind if she thinks this is one.

Uma looks at him, then at Mama. 'We haven't had any for so long,' she says apologetically. 'Ramu has come after such a long time —'

Ramu beams at her as she bends to pour his tea. 'Yes, but I will stay a long time to make up for that,' he assures her and, in the manner in which he glances at his elderly relatives, it is hard not to detect a certain mischief.

Certainly they believe it is out of mischief

that he uses up all the hot water in the hamam for his bath, then asks if there aren't any chops or cutlets for breakfast in addition to the puris, and insists on telling them ribald stories about respected aunts and uncles that neither Mama or Papa want to hear, till he falls asleep on the divan in the drawing room and lies there all morning without thought for the guests that might drop in — even if they do not. In the evening, instead of settling down on the veranda to play a game of cards with his uncle and aunt, he shows a restlessness that is almost like a physical itch. He clumps up and down the terrace in his heavy boots, with a tense air, clasping and unclasping his hands behind his back, now and then running his fingers through his hair and making it stand on end, wiry and streaked with premature grey.

Even Uma becomes uneasy. All through her childhood she has heard whispered gossip about Bakul Uncle's son: some thought it was drink, others drugs. This is clearly on her parents' minds as well; they refuse to talk any more. Their questions about Bakul Uncle, Lila Aunty and cousin Anamika have been ignored, or answered briefly and perfunctorily.

'Father works all day, mother goes to

lunch parties and plays cards. And Anamika
—' thinking of his beautiful and good and
loved sister, he gives a small, somewhat
wistful smile. 'She wins all the prizes,' he
winds up abruptly.

Uma breaks into the silence that follows.

'Shall we go across and visit the neighbours, Ramu-bhai?' Uma suggests. She
thinks he might be offered a little whisky
and water there: she knows Uncle Joshi is
partial to a drink in the evenings, especially
if there are visitors.

'No. But Uma, listen. Let's go out. Come
on, come on. Yes, yes, you must.' Her suggestion seems to have set a match to dry
tinder; he is on fire to get away. 'I'll take you
out to dinner,' he offers grandly, throwing
out an arm in invitation.

Papa and Mama's mouths fall open —
their lips and tongues look white. Uma
squeaks, 'To dinner?' in utter disbelief.

'Yes, can't one get dinner anywhere in this
city? There must be a restaurant —'

'There's Kwality's!' Uma cries suddenly,
making her parents turn their faces from
Ramu to her without altering their thunderstruck expressions: what could she be
thinking of, suggesting dinner in a restaurant? She has never been to one in her life;
how can she think of starting now when her

hair is already grey.

Then Papa gathers himself together. It is up to him to prevent this situation from getting completely out of control. 'No need to waste money by eating at Kwality's,' he says sternly. 'No need. Waste! Kwality's — bah!'

'Dinner has been prepared at home,' Mama adds, also coming to life.

'No, no, we must eat out. I insist. I will take Uma out to dinner. The best dinner we can get in this city. Isn't there an hotel, with a bar?'

Even Uma is shocked. 'Ramu-bhai,' she says in warning.

But although the parents are stuttering in alarm and outrage, and protesting as furiously as a band of mynahs in the thick of disagreement, Ramu is not to be deflected. 'Can't I take my cousin out for dinner? Didn't you once send me to fetch her the time she ran away?' he reminds them of an intimacy they would have preferred to forget. 'Wasn't I the one who brought her back?' He is pulling Uma to her feet, he is pushing her to go and get ready, he is shouting through the door to hurry her, he has called the mali, who was phlegmatically weeding a corner of the lawn, to go and fetch a rickshaw and — right under the parents' scandalised noses — he has ridden off with her and is waving back with an infuriating insouciance, the insouciance of the black sheep who has nothing to lose, calling, 'Bye-bye! See you! Good night!' and even 'Ta-ta!'

Uma and Ramu are propping themselves up on the slippery red rexine seats of a booth in the Carlton Hotel's dining room. All the other customers have left. It is late. The waiters lean against the stucco pillars, picking at their ears or their noses, and yawning. But Ramu and Uma do not notice. Ramu summons one with a snap of his fingers and hands him a scrap of paper — one of the bills for drinks that he has been accumulating in a saucer at his elbow and on which he has scribbled something with a ball-point pen — with the instruction, 'Take this to the bandmaster. Tell him to play "My Darling Clementine" for us.' The waiter slouches across to where the musicians, seated on a small podium, are wiping their instruments, talking to each other, in tired voices, ready to pack up and leave. The bandmaster looks across at them, quite evidently with loathing. Ramu waves at him cheerily and calls across encouragingly, 'You're a great band, a great band! You should be playing in Bombay — at the Taj!'

74

They feel obliged then to strike up and prove him right, but their instruments sound like cutlery being washed and flung into a drawer at the end of a party.

Ramu cocks an eyebrow at Uma and sings, 'O my darlin', O my darlin', O my darlin' Clementine. . . .'

Uma rolls against the red rexine seat, her hair escaping in long strands from the steel pins that usually keep it knotted tightly in place. It lies untidily about her cheeks and neck. Behind the thick lenses of her spectacles, her eyes roll in time to the music. She takes another sip of the shandy Ramu has insisted she drink and hiccups like a drunkard in a farce about fallen women.

'Oh, Ramu-bhai,' she hiccups, 'you are so-o fun-ee!'

'I am so fun-ee,' he sings the line, improvising to the tune of 'My Darling Clementine'. 'I am a bunn-ee —'

'Ra-mu!' Uma squeals, spluttering into her glass.

'Hop, hop, hop,' warbles Ramu, making his fingers dance across the tabletop towards her.

'Stop, Ramu, stop!'

'Stop, stop, stop,' he sings, making his fingers dance backwards. 'Funny bunny, funny bunny.'

Uma is choking with laughter. She has laughed so much, she has tears in her eyes. They run down her cheeks.

'Don't cry, Uma,' Ramu breaks off to say in concern. 'You remember I looked after you when you ran away, I fetched you home that time? I want you to enjoy yourself. Have another drink.' He snaps his fingers at a waiter who has propped himself up against the bar and will not move. 'Waiter!' he calls again, 'another round!'

His voice rings out across the restaurant, unexpectedly loud because at that moment the band has stopped playing. The musicians are laying down their instruments with an air of finality. 'Oh, no,' Ramu calls, 'don't do that. Come on, play us another tune. Look, you've still got customers here, you can't go away.' He is standing on his feet, leaning forwards against the table. 'Come on, play us a tune. We want to dance. Play "She'll Be Coming 'Round the Mountain" —'

But the musicians pretend not to hear. They are packing up their instruments, shuffling out. Only the bandmaster turns to wave at them. 'Bye-bye,' he calls, 'cheerio!' He won't listen to Ramu's pleas, or threats. Then the lights go off — snap, snap, snap. A waiter is coming towards them, flapping his napkin about as if to sweep them away with the crumbs.

They stand on the pavement together, bits of cigarette paper and cinema tickets and empty icecream cups at their feet. Uma is crying because the evening is over, Ramu is trying to find a bicycle rickshaw. They are riding past him, refusing to stop because it is late and they are on their way home. He has to take out a ten rupee note and wave it over his head, there under the lamppost, before one agrees to take them all the way to the Civil Lines at this time of night. They climb in and Ramu holds onto Uma's arm. 'Uma, Uma,' he calls into her ear because she seems to be so far away, 'remember funny bunny? Funny bunny, Uma?'

She giggles then and they are still giggling when they fall out of the rickshaw at the gate where the mali stands waiting for them, a small withered man with a giant-sized flash-light in his hand, having been ordered to do so by Papa who is pacing up and down on the terrace and comes thundering towards them with a face as black as the night.

'Get into the house, you two!' he hisses at them. 'Get in at once!'

'Yes, uncle, we are getting into the house, we have come to get into the house,' Ramu tries to placate him, but finds himself being manhandled towards the door where Mama is waiting in her white night sari.

Uma finds herself grasped by the shoulder and pushed into her room so that her handbag and her flowers fall out of her hands. Still, she insists on turning around and telling her mother, 'I had shandy to drink, Mama — and the band played — and Ramu and I danced —'

'Quiet, you hussy! Not another word from you, you idiot child!' Mama's face glints like a knife in the dark, growing narrower and fiercer as it comes closer. 'You, you disgrace to the family — nothing but disgrace, *ever!*'

Uma had failed somehow to notice, on Mira-masi's visits, that her aunt was growing older rapidly, that her youthful energy and her glossy black hair (that seemed to Mama — and many other relatives — such an affront in a widow) were no longer what they had been. Her face began to look muddy and was streaked with deep lines like a river bed that has run dry, and her hair was turning thin and grey. Of course she still wore her widow's garments of white, she still performed the same rituals, and even continued to make milk and sugar treats for the family, but all a little less enthusiastically, less energetically.

She was unpacking her altar objects with a tired sigh when Uma noticed, and cried out, 'But where is your Lord, masi?' for the familiar brass figure, rubbed smooth over the years, was missing. Mira-masi's lips crumpled into a crease of sorrow, 'Stolen, child,' she muttered, 'stolen from me on my last pilgrimage to Rishikesh. Can you believe that one pilgrim would steal from another? And that, too, God's image? That is what happens in this kala-yuga, this dark age,' and she struck her forehead with the heel of her palm, so hard that Uma was awe-struck by the force. 'But I will get it back,' Mira-masi vowed, striking once again, still harder. 'I will travel to every place of pilgrimage, every temple and ashram, till I find the one who stole it from me, and get it back. I won't rest till I have my Lord back,' and her eyes glittered with both rage and a fervent desire that made Uma draw back, frightened: she had known how important the image was to Mira-masi, but had not understood the quality of her passion.

From now on Mira-masi's pilgrimages were less the holiday excursions they had been, visiting relatives on the way, carrying

79

family gossip from one to the other, staying on for weddings or a pleasant spell of weather. Now she seemed to storm through the country, stomping along the pilgrim routes, her back bowed, a staff in her hands, her large feet plodding grimly and determinedly the worn earth of those paths.

Once she came to them quite ill, and gaunt. She lay on her rush mat, feverish, getting up only for the ritual ceremonies. She was on her way to an ashram in the foothills. Mama tried to dissuade her — 'There are no doctors there, no medicines' — but her mind was set. What she said was, 'I will get better there. Let Uma come and help. Let Uma come with me.' Uma heard her, and her eyes went round as those of a fish, with disbelief, but Mama was caught in a trap: having voiced concern, now she could not refuse; and Uma was allowed to go.

On the bus, Mira-masi revived. She was clearly in her element now. She ordered the other passengers to make room for Uma. She cajoled them into letting her bring a little bundle of belongings into the bus with her instead of tying it up on top along with the others' tin trunks and baskets and bedding rolls. She leant out of the window and beckoned the fruit seller and the peanut vendor and bought provisions to share with Uma and their fellow passengers. When the bus finally lurched into motion and trundled on its way, she even burst into an excited shout of 'Har har Mahadev!' The others were so infected by her enthusiasm that they echoed the call, over and over, in triumphant shouts, and Uma was so embarrassed that her own throat refused to utter any sound at all. It was soon parched as well, with thirst and dust and the heat of the bus, not to speak of the unfamiliarity of the situation itself which would never have come up in the world presided over by MamaPapa. She reminded herself of its uniqueness, its adventurousness, trying to use that to repel the onset of travel sickness to which she was prone and which engulfed her now. But she was not strong enough and failed to defeat it and reduce it to the illusion that Mira-masi assured her it was for true pilgrims. Instead, she had to climb across Mira-masi's knees and lean out of the bus window to vomit, ignominiously, into the dusty ditch along the road. Mira-masi did not even pretend to sympathise, she was so horrified by the uncleanliness, the pollution. 'We must bathe at once, we must find a tap and bathe,' she said agitatedly, and covered her nose with the end of her sari while Uma tried to wipe herself clean and become somehow less revolting. The bus did stop every now and then, not at a tap where they might wash but to collect more and more passengers — there were now people practically sitting on their laps, and necks and shoulders as well. The heat of midday circulated amongst them sluggishly. The bus seemed barely able to proceed, it was so overloaded with people and luggage, and there were more people with more objects on the street to prevent them from proceeding even if it could have done.

Nevertheless, they did arrive, late in the afternoon, and were disgorged at a bus depot in the middle of a bazaar that looked exactly like the bazaars and depots at all the towns they had passed on the way. But Mira-masi recognised the place, and knew exactly what to do. Hailing a tonga hitched to the sorriest nag of all in a row of shabby, decrepit carriages over which flies hummed and hovered as if they were edible, she climbed in with Uma and their baggage, and directed the driver to the ashram. Uma sat clutching at the awning, and concentrating on keeping from sliding off the narrow sloping seat made her wakeful. The open carriage at least admitted air freely even if that was foetid and polluted with the exhaust of buses and motor rickshaws that roared around them. It was not very often that she rode in a tonga and she found the bumpy, rattling drive exhilarating, although Mira-masi had lowered her face into a fold of her sari and refused to look at the driver — with his short beard dyed red with henna and a small embroidered cap on his head, he was evidently a Muslim — or the leather whip he wielded over the nag's sore and skeletal haunches, and Uma heard her muttering 'Hari Om' under her breath as if to keep away the devils of pollution. 'Are you all right?' Uma enquired, now fit enough to look after her. 'This is *fun,*' she added encouragingly, only to have Mira-masi roll her eyes at her, appalled.

Yet the tonga did get them out of the town and to the ashram, and from the relief in Mira-masi's eyes, voice and gestures, Uma understood that there were no more rigours to be faced. The gatekeeper seemed to recognise Mira-masi for he opened the tall sky-blue iron gates to her, and even carried their bundles to the ashram buildings which lay scattered around a large courtyard at the foot of low, scrubby hills. There was no one else around, just a yellow bitch sleeping in the shade of some pink-flowering oleanders. The temple at one end of the courtyard was brightly painted pink and blue and green but seemed deserted. Mira-masi went straight up a gravel path neatly edged with shrubs to the long low building with its deep veranda and flat roof shaded by an immense banyan tree in which parakeets were contentedly picking at berries and scattering them down in the dust.

This was where Mira-masi and Uma were to stay, together, in a room at the end of the veranda. The room was bare. It had a cement floor on which they set down their bags. There was a broom propped up in a corner with which to keep it clean. Outside, on the veranda, stood an earthen jar of drinking water. Every morning the water carrier would fill it with water from the river below, down at the edge of a path that twisted through the scrub and rocks of the low dun hills, across the sand to the riverbed where a narrow green channel of water ran between parched clay. Enormous fishing eagles circled languidly in the sky above the still landscape. Only during the morning and evening prayers was there a beating of cymbals and ringing of bells and a coming together of people on the temple precincts. For the rest of the day there was silence.

Mira-masi sat cross-legged on the veranda, holding her string of wooden beads in her hands, her lips moving soundlessly. When fever overtook her, she went in and lay down on the mat she had spread on the floor, and her lips continued to murmur prayers till she fell asleep. Only occasionally did she open her eyes and glance at Uma, almost as if she were surprised by her presence. Uma was perfectly happy not to be noticed. She had never been more unsupervised or happier in her life.

Uma was expected to join the others — priests, pilgrims, widows — and sit in a row on the floor to eat the rice and vegetables they were served. She would have preferred to take her food out under the tree and eat alone — she was the only young person there — but this was clearly not possible: Mira-masi's look told her so.

Sometimes she trailed along with Mira-masi to the temple for the evening prayers and sat on the terrace for a while, listening to a priest with blazing, fanatical eyes, play the harmonium and lead the others in singing impassioned hymns:

'O blow the conch,
Light the incense,
As the Lord,
Holding fire in his hand,
Dances to the sound of the drum,
On the burning ground . . .'

Uma tried not to look into the priest's
face, or listen to the words of the hymn either: there was an air of abandonment about
them that made her feel uneasily as if
MamaPapa, those enemies of abandon,
were standing behind her and watching her
and all of them, with scorn. She was reminded of the time she had run to the convent and Sister Teresa had brought her back
to deposit her with Mama, and Mama's
rage. She felt uneasily caught once more between powerful forces pulling in different
directions, and it was no good looking to
Mira-masi for guidance; her guidance
would clearly lead only to trouble.

Fortunately, for most of the day, she was
left to herself and spent it in wandering
down to the river. It was too hot during the
day to venture out across the baking sand to
the water, but it could be approached very
early in the morning when the light was still
pale and translucent, or in the evening when
the sun withdrew and a little breeze stirred.

Otherwise she stayed on the hillside where she picked berries too hard and green to eat, watched insects making their way across the path and into cracks, or sat in the sparse shade of a thorny grey tree and watched the fishing eagles soar into the vast sky.

On a distant spur, an ancient grizzled hermit had built himself an underground cave in which he lived, and Uma sometimes crept half-way to it to spy, then lost nerve and ran all the way back in a panic.

When she returned, usually late in the evening after hours of walking barefoot through the sand along the river, Mira-masi looked at her as if she did not recognise her. Once she seized her by the shoulders, held her down, kneeling in front of her, and stared into her mud-smeared face, at the sandy streaming hair and torn, stained clothes of the child. Her eyes narrowed, and Uma flinched, expecting a reprimand.

Instead, Mira-masi whispered, through dry lips, 'You are the Lord's child. The Lord has chosen you. You bear His mark.'

Uma was much more terrified than if Mira-masi had merely threatened her with punishment for staying out so late. Perhaps she was also giddy from too much sun, too little food. Perhaps Mira-masi's stare was hypnotic. In any case, she found she could not stir. She knelt, gazing back into Mira-masi's eyes, held down by her shoulders, and began to tremble. Shooting pains crept up from her knees. She tried to draw away, to throw herself on the ground. Mira-masi held on, making Uma pull away more strongly so that she succeeded in falling. Agitatedly, the woman tried to lift Uma but Uma made herself rigid. She had turned quite cold. She clenched her teeth together and bit her tongue so that the blood ran, lurid, scarlet. She began to roll on the floor, from side to side, throwing her head about and moaning, while Mira-masi tried to hold her, crying, 'Child, child.'

Some of the priests, who had been pacing in the courtyard, heard and came at a run. They found Uma on the floor, rolling and tossing her head and drumming her heels, Mira-masi helpless and awed.

They were frightened. They stood at the door, crying in alarm.

Mira-masi said, 'She is possessed. The Lord has taken possession of her.'

Uma let out a shriek on hearing this, and the shriek continued for so long that her face went blue, then purple. She could not stop. She could not get her breath back. It was leaving her, in one long, shrill exhalation.

The others stood watching, enthralled.

Then the priests at the door were suddenly bundled aside. The pilgrim who lived in the room at the other end of the long veranda, bustled in. Seeing Uma blue and purple on the floor and fighting for breath, he bent and lifted her up as if she were an infant newly born, and struck her on the back, banged and thwacked her with a mighty arm. He had been a doctor once and given up his practice in Calcutta to learn and then teach yoga, but now he was a gynaecologist again, delivering an absent woman of a reluctant child. And, like a baby, Uma gasped with shock, and so drew in a breath. Then another gasp, another breath. Her lungs began to pump again. She was compelled to breathe. She hung over the doctor's dark, muscular arm, gulping air.

She had an audience. They all watched her, open-mouthed, till suddenly Uma was very sick, all over the floor.

Then they scattered, Mira-masi shrieking, 'Tchh! Oof! Aré!' and Uma sank down on the floor, mortified.

They became very respectful of Uma now, watchful and curious. She was still the only young person at the ashram — and they could not deny she was childish when they saw her laughing at the monkeys up in the banyan tree or eating green berries from the bushes on the hillside — but they became shy of treating her as one, or even of speaking to her. When she followed Mira-masi to the temple at her request, the head priest beckoned to her, inviting her to come in. Uma drew back and dropped the end of Mira-masi's sari which she was holding. So they let her be, but the young priest who played the harmonium gazed directly at her when he sang, and his voice was no longer steady but quavered emotionally:

> 'My eyes see the golden form
> Of my Lord,
> And the crescent moon shining
> Amidst his tresses.
> Joy wells up in my heart,
> As honey in a lotus . . .'

Uma looked down at her knees. She scratched at a scab there till Mira-masi nudged her. Then she lowered her knees, tried to sit still, and stared up at the ceiling that was painted blue and from which strands of tinsel and faded paper streamers dangled as if left over from a birthday party.

At night she lay quietly on her mat, listening to the ashram dog bark. Then other dogs — in distant villages, out along the river bed and over in the pampas grass, or in wayside shacks and hovels by the highway — barked back. They howled long messages to each other. Their messages travelled back and forth through the night darkness which was total, absolute. Gradually the barks sank into it and drowned. Then it was silent. That was what Uma felt her own life to have been — full of barks, howls, messages, and now — silence.

The gate to the ashram opened. A tonga had drawn up. Out of it unfolded two dusty, bedraggled figures, one large, the other small. One limped forward, the other hopped. They came up the gravel path. They were Ramu and Arun.

Throwing his bag down on the steps, Ramu sank down, grey-faced. Mopping his face with a filthy handkerchief, he told the speechless Uma sourly, 'I've come to take you back. Couldn't you find a better time to run away than in the middle of summer?'

'Uma!' screeched Arun from the other end of the veranda. 'See, monkeys in the tree! Have you a catapult?'

Mira-masi held her head in her hands. 'Now what is this? Who has sent them? Who told them to come here?'

Uma stood wrapped around the stucco pillar of the veranda, tongue-tied as she tried to disentangle her delight at seeing her cousin Ramu from her embarrassment at being the cause of his distress. 'I — don't — know, I — don't — know,' she mumbled to Mira-masi. Then asked Ramu, 'Ramu-bhai, *who* sent you to fetch me? I haven't run away. I'm here.'

'I can see you're here,' he told her. 'I only wish you weren't. Then I wouldn't have been sent all this way by bus and tonga by your Papa to bring you back.'

'Back? Why?' she faltered, knitting her hands around the pillar. She had quite forgotten that she was expected to return.

'Because your MamaPapa thought you would be back in a week and you have been away for a month. When I arrived for what I hoped would be a bit of a holiday, they were all howling and crying. They were sure you'd been abducted by the priests.'

'What's *abducted?*' Uma asked cautiously.

'Stolen. Kidnapped. Ravished!' he shouted. 'All that. And I have been sent to rescue you. Don't ask why it had to be me and not your father. I suppose he couldn't travel by bus and tonga — he'd lose face. Next time you run away or get abducted, make sure it's to a place on the railway line.'

Uma threw frightened looks at Mira-masi who was frowning. She did not understand Ramu's English but she was clever at following the drift of a conversation. She seemed to guess what he asserted by his tone. She was folding her arms, tucking her feet beneath her, preparing for battle. She was not going to be beaten by this English-speaking, meat-eating, polluted outcast from Bombay. But he simply ignored her and spoke to Uma. 'Go and get me some water, there's a good girl,' he said. 'Don't you see your old cousin's about to collapse? And silence that brother of yours, will you? He's been enough of a nuisance all through the journey.' He looked bitterly in the direction of Arun who was running around the banyan tree in search of a stick to throw at the monkeys.

Uma was relieved to be given a task and hurried to fetch a glass and pour water from the jar for Ramu. He took it from her, closed his eyes, and emptied it over his head so that the water ran through his hair and into his eyes and dripped down his nose and chin into his collar. Uma, remembering now why Ramu had always been her favourite cousin, shrieked with laughter. She held her middle with folded arms and doubled up and hooted with laughter.

Mira-masi sat as if she had been turned to stone. Disapproval of Ramu made her mouth tighten as if around some sour, un-ripe fruit. But finally she sent Uma off to silence Arun before anyone started com-plaining about the noise he was making. While Uma was away, she would deal with Ramu, her look said.

The battle raged all afternoon. It was mostly silent, conducted by grimaces and gestures, an occasional sharp, exasperated word. Ramu drooped and now and then rolled his eyes upwards to express his feel-ings. Mira-masi remained bolt upright, her hands folded on her lap, her lips folded into her chin, shooting looks like fiery arrows from under brows that were drawn bows. But whenever Uma slipped in or out, frightenedly glancing at them, Ramu would make a face at her — thumb his nose or stick out his tongue, and even pretend to pour an invisible glass of water over his head. This reduced her to giggles, and, armed with her giggles, Ramu won.

Uma found herself being handed into the bicycle rickshaw the gate-keeper had hailed to take them to the bus depot. What with the trouble of finding room for three passengers on the single narrow seat, and loading their baggage on as well, there was no time for farewells or leavetaking. They were already pedalling out of the sky-blue gate and down the road in a whirl of grey dust when Uma realised she had been taken away from Mira-masi and the ashram and river and was on her way home. She tried to get up in her agitation and jump off.

Ramu shouted, 'Sit *down*, Uma. D'you want me to deal with broken heads and legs as well?' Then, seeing her face so bereft, he dropped his threatening manner and said contritely, 'You look starved. We'll stop and have some samosas at the depot before we get on the bus.'

'Samosas?' Arun yelled. 'Ya-ay!' He, too, was a boy on holiday.

Uma made a polite attempt to eat them while Ramu smiled at her encouragingly. He held them out to her on a piece of news-paper — a peace offering, a consolation — but her throat was dry, nothing could pass through it. She looked back at him dumbly and Arun ate her share.

Six

It is years since Mama had any new jewellery made but the old jeweller still comes around every winter to unwrap his bundle, take out his boxes and open them before her in the hope of tantalising her beyond the point where she can refuse.

Mama always does begin by refusing but then tells Uma to go and fetch the gold bangles or a broken chain. He looks up from tying his boxes and bundles together and smiles joyfully, his betel-stained teeth juicy in his mouth. 'Am I to make Baby's wedding jewellery this year?' he asks. He has been making the same joke since she was two years old. On each visit, they have found each other greyer, older. Now he can hardly see through the spectacles which he has done up with tape and string so he can hook them onto his nose.

He sits in a corner of the veranda, on a white cloth Mama has had spread for him, bent over his instruments and his little lamp, turning an armband into four thin gold bangles, or else putting together four thin gold bangles into one armband, whatever Mama's whim dictates. She sits on the swing, rocking, watching him, humming at the sight of the shining metal she loves so dearly, and Uma sits mending Mama's petticoats or knitting a sweater for Arun — more practical, she thinks, than the shawl Mama has sent to protect him from the cold of the Massachusetts winter — occasionally glancing in the direction of its golden allure. Sometimes she gets up to go and fetch him a glass of tea.

Placing it on the floor beside him, he beams at her and cackles, 'And the wedding jewellery for Baby? Am I to make it *this* year?' Uma can never control the blush that reddens her face, and she sniffs, 'Don't talk nonsense. Such an old man, and still talking nonsense!'

❦

There was a time, a season, when every girl in the big, farflung family seemed suddenly ready for marriage. It was as if their mothers had been tending them, in their flowerpots, for just this moment when their cheeks would fill out and their lips take on a glisten and all the giggles and whispers would arrive at that one decision — *marriage*.

As anyone might have predicted — and aunts and grandmothers had been doing for years — it was cousin Anamika who was the first fruit to be picked. Cousin Anamika, in distant Bombay, had seemed the blessed one of her generation from her birth onwards, and it was not just because she presented such a startling contrast to her misshapen, deformed, dark misfortune of a brother, Ramu, with his club foot, his hunched back, his nearly sightless eyes — a son, a child who had gone wrong, missed all the graces and gifts that were accorded instead to his sister. Nor was it just a matter of her beauty. Aruna was pretty too, and in her case it was also evident quite early that her future would be bright, but there was a sharp edge to her prettiness, a harsh edge given to it by a kind of steely determination, a dogged ambitiousness, that seemed to be born of a desperation. In Anamika there was no such thing: she was simply lovely as a flower is lovely, soft, petal-skinned, bumblebee-eyed, pink-lipped, always on the verge of bubbling dove-like laughter, loving smiles, and with a good nature like a radiance about her. Wherever she was, there was peace, contentment, well-being.

When she was small, her parents would bring her on visits; not very often because Bakul Uncle's practice in Bombay was such a thriving one, he could scarcely ever leave the city to visit his more plodding, less spectacular younger brother who had preferred to be a big frog in the little well of a small provincial town rather than risk the challenges of a metropolis. This created a certain air of rivalry and mutual censure whenever they came together which was obediently echoed by their wives and made these visits a fraught occasion; and there would be fierce competition between Uma and Aruna as well, for Anamika's attention. Uma would link arms with her cousin to lead her to her room to show off her collection of Christmas cards, and Aruna would try to snatch at her hand and take her out shopping for glass bangles. If Uma wanted to stroll with her in the garden where the bed of roses bloomed briefly in the cool of winter — the only season when Bakul Uncle and Lila Aunty would consider visiting them — then Aruna wanted to take her indoors and show her all the clothes in her wardrobe. Somehow Anamika managed to please them both, smile at all their suggestions, accept them with an equal readiness. She never allowed herself to be pulled into one camp or another; she achieved this equilibrium by simply remaining at the centre, so that everyone had to come to her, attracted to her as bees to a lotus. A lotus, with her deep, creamy, still beauty — that was what she was. Or a pearl, smooth and luminous.

Sometimes they met in other towns, at family weddings to which relatives from all the corners of the land came streaming, happy to display their richest silks and jewels to each other. Then a little group formed of just their generation, and rampaged through the wedding marquee, drinking as many soft drinks as they could lay their hands on, eating enough sweets to make an elephant sick; and always it was Anamika who prevented them from going too far, not by words or a look, but simply by her example which was cool, poised, mannerly and graceful. Wherever Anamika was, there was moderation, good sense and calm.

Even the adults looked on Anamika's

glossy head, her thick dark braids and her big dreamy eyes, and smiled, sometimes sadly as if thinking how their own daughters and daughters-in-law could never measure up to this blessed one. Many observed how Ramu seemed to have drawn all misfortune upon himself so nothing but good fortune could look upon his sister. Uncles and grandfathers liked to have Anamika near them, ask her about her school and studies, for it was the astonishing truth that Anamika was not only pretty, and good, but an outstanding student as well.

In fact, she did so brilliantly in her final school exams, that she won a scholarship to Oxford. To Oxford, where only the most favoured and privileged sons could ever hope to go! Naturally her parents would not countenance her actually going abroad to study — just when she was of an age to marry — everyone understood that, and agreed, and so the letter of acceptance from Oxford was locked in a steel cupboard in their flat on Marine Drive in Bombay, and whenever visitors came, it would be taken out and shown around with pride. The visitors would congratulate Anamika and she would look down at her lap and play with the end of her braid and say nothing at all. She could never bring herself to contradict her parents or cause them grief.

The scholarship was one of the qualifications they were able to offer when they started searching for a husband for her, and it was what won her a husband who was considered an equal to this prize of the family.

Then why, at that moment, when triumph should have reached its apogee, did everything change? And all good fortune veer around and plunge shockingly downwards?

In a way, it was Anamika's scholarship that had summoned him up, brought him to her parents' attention out of the swarm of other suitors, because he had qualifications equal to hers; he too had degrees, had won medals and certificates, and it seemed clear he would be a match for her.

Uma, Aruna and all the other girl cousins crowded around to see the match when he came, a bridegroom, to the wedding, and they fell back when they saw him, in dismay. He was so much older than Anamika, so grim-faced and conscious of his own superiority to everyone else present: those very degrees and medals had made him insufferably proud and kept everyone at a distance. The children saw that straight away: there would be no bridegroom jokes played at this wedding, no little gifts and bribes from him to them. In fact, he barely noticed them; he barely seemed to notice Anamika. The children saw that too — that she was marrying the one person who was totally impervious to Anamika's beauty and grace and distinction. He was too occupied with maintaining his superiority. He raised his chin and his nose — which was as long and sharp as a needle — and seemed to look over the top of her head as they exchanged heavy garlands of rose and jasmine, then sat before the ceremonial fire. The children twisted and squirmed to see what it was that he was staring at: was there a mirror hanging a little above the bride's head in which he could see himself?

Yes, in a way there was: it was the face of his mother, as sharp-nosed and grim-featured as he, gazing steadily back at him with an expression of fortitude in the face of calamity. They were to find out that this was how it was — it was the relationship central to his life, leaving room for no other. Anamika was simply an interloper, someone brought in because it was the custom and because she would, by marrying him, enhance his superiority to other men. So they had to tolerate her.

Only they did not tolerate her. No one said so openly, but Uma and Aruna heard gossip, over the next year or two, whispers and low voices that dropped even lower when they were within earshot. When they did pick up some hints, some information, it was deeply troubling: Anamika had been beaten, Anamika was beaten regularly by her mother-in-law while her husband stood by and approved — or, at least, did not object. Anamika spent her entire time in the kitchen, cooking for his family which was large so that meals were eaten in shifts — first the men, then the children, finally the women. She herself ate the remains in the pots before scouring them (or did Uma and Aruna imagine this last detail?). If the pots were not properly scoured, so they heard, her mother-in-law threw them on the ground and made her do them all over again. When Anamika was not scrubbing or cooking, she was in her mother-in-law's room, either massaging that lady's feet or folding and tidying her clothes. She never went out of the house except to the temple with other women. Anamika had never once been out alone with her husband. Aruna wondered what she did with all the fine clothes and jewellery she had been given at her wedding.

Then the news came that Anamika had had to go to the hospital. She had had a miscarriage at home, it was said, after a beating. It was said she could not bear more children. Now Anamika was flawed, she was damaged goods. She was no longer perfect. Would she be sent back to her family? Everyone waited to hear.

Uma said, 'I hope they will send her back. Then she will be home with Lila Aunty again, and happy.'

'You are so silly, Uma,' Mama snapped as she whacked at a mosquito on her foot with the small palm-leaf fan she was waving. 'How can she be happy if she is sent home? What will people say? What will they think?'

While Uma gaped, trying to think of something to say that would strike down Mama's silly thoughts as her fan struck down the mosquito, Aruna cried out for her instead, 'Who cares what they say? Who cares what they think?'

'Don't talk like that,' Mama scolded them. 'I don't want to hear all these modern ideas. Is it what you learnt from the nuns at the convent?' She glared at Uma; Mother Agnes had made one of her periodic visits to persuade Mama to send Uma back to school and this always roused Mama's ire. Uma thought it better to withdraw. So then

Mama glared at Aruna. 'All this convent education — what good does it do? Better to marry you off than let you go to *that* place.' She laid about her with the palm-leaf fan.

Mama's temper was bad that summer — some female problem was mentioned, one with a long name, when female friends or relatives visited — but Aruna simply swung her foot, toyed with her braid and rippled with an inner momentum.

Seven

Uma has been sent through the hedge to the neighbours with a message from Mama — one of those requests for a knitting pattern or a magazine that she often sends across — and Uma finds Mrs Joshi in her kitchen, one end of her sari tucked in at the waist, making icecream. Or, rather, overseeing a servant boy who is grinding away at the handle of a wooden tub. She waves when she sees Uma approach. 'Just in time — the icecream's nearly ready — don't go away without tasting it.' Uma immediately hastens her steps and comes over, smiling in anticipation. She too watches the boy turn the handle and listens to the ice crackle and crunch till the lid is lifted off and Mrs Joshi dips in her spoon to test it for thickness. She too cries out with pleasure when it is declared done. Mrs Joshi fills a little pink glass dish for Uma. Then she stands with her hands on her hips and watches Uma eat it up, so fast, in such quick gulps, that Mrs Joshi has to fill it a second time. Uma finishes that also and licks the spoon clean before putting it down beside the empty dish. She hands it over to the servant boy who has been watching her with a twist of a grin on his face.

When Uma has left, Mrs Joshi turns to the old widowed aunt who lives with them and has come to see if there is anything good going in the kitchen. 'That Uma,' she says, shaking her head a little, 'still like a child of six. Won't she ever grow up, poor thing?'

The servant boy makes a snorting sound at the sink where he is washing up, and Mrs Joshi swings around to reprimand him.

∞

It was during the sad aftermath of Anamika's marriage that all the relatives received letters from Papa to say, 'Uma is still young but may be considered of marriageable age and we see no reason to continue her studies beyond class eight —'; Papa had not informed them when Uma was withdrawn from school well before that level. The letter rippled through the ranks of the female relatives. Everywhere there was a gathering of forces. Then the ripples made their way back to the source. Some of their replies enclosed photographs of likely young men known to aunts and cousins in distant towns. Uma was shown them (a sign of the family's progressiveness). Aruna hung over her shoulder and pointed out that the tall one had spectacles and thinning hair and the fat one had bad teeth and hair that was greasy. Uma tried to shake her off, irritated by this criticism of her suitors, but she could not deny — and was rather frightened to see — that all of them bore glum, disgruntled expressions. For some reason that was not divulged to her, one of them was picked and invited to visit them along with his sister and brother-in-law who lived in the same town and even knew their neighbour, Mrs Joshi (in fact, it was she who had procured the photograph, unknown to Uma).

Mama lent one of her own saris to Uma for the occasion — a cream georgette with little sprigs of pink and blue roses embroidered all along the border. ('Old-fashioned!' sniffed Aruna. 'A granny sari!') She also did Uma's plaits up in a roll on her neck and stuck a pink flower into the roll with a long pin. 'We should powder your face a little,' she said, peering into Uma's face with an expression of dissatisfaction. 'It might cover some of the pimples. Why have you got so many pimples today? They weren't there yesterday,' she accused her.

'I get new ones all the time, Mama,' Uma said, then cried 'Ow!' as Mama rubbed some of them too hard with a flat powder puff that smelt unpleasantly of stale perspiration.

'Hold still. You have to look nice,' Mama said grimly.

'Why, Mama?' Uma squirmed, and shut her eyes as clouds of powder flew around, ferociously scented. 'It is only Joshi Aunty's friend —'

'*And* her brother from Kanpur,' Mama added significantly. 'He is in the leather business,' and she scrubbed at Uma's face as if it were a piece of hide to be offered for examination.

But it was not only leather goods that were being proffered; Uma must present other accomplishments as well. 'Now if Mrs Syal asks if *you* made the samosas, you must say *yes*.'

'Samosas!' squealed Uma, her hand flying to the most magnetic of the pimples now that Mama had stopped scrubbing at them.

'Yes, we are having samosas for tea, and barfi.'

'I made barfi also?'

'You *did*,' Mama threatened her with a fierce look. All this work, and nothing to show for it — that was Mama's fate. How Mama had always envied Lila Aunty for having a daughter like Anamika, a model of perfection like Anamika. No, that was not for her, she sighed.

'What if she asks me how? I won't know!' Uma cried.

'*Why* don't you know? Didn't I tell you to go to the kitchen and learn these things? For so many years I have been telling you, and did you listen? No, you were at the convent, singing those Christian hymns. You were playing games with that Anglo-Indian teacher showing you how to wear skirts and jump around. Play, play, play, that is all you ever did. Will that help you now?'

Uma would have protested if her mother had not been manhandling her quite roughly, pushing very small bangles over her large hands and onto her wrists, and even shoving her own small ruby ring onto her finger. Uma had always loved that ruby ring and tried to submit to the torture without crying, but when she looked at the swollen finger and the bluish lump caused by its tightness, she could not help worrying how she would pull it off after the tea party was over.

All through that painful afternoon, she sat trying to tear it off her finger. When her mother threw her a warning look from behind the tea tray, she stopped for a few minutes, then started again, desperately. To begin with, the visitors' attention was directed respectfully towards the mother but when it eventually came to rest, as it had to, on Uma, the girl's frantic movements could not be ignored. Finally, Mrs Syal, a large young woman who had eyed every item of Uma's clothing very closely, said, 'It is a nice ring.'

Uma, looking down at it as if it were the first time she had seen it, went red all over her face and gasped, 'My mother's.'

'Have another barfi, Mrs Syal,' said Mama, and persuaded Uma to get up and pass the plate with the sweets around again.

'Mmm, nice,' said Mrs Syal, picking up another and examining it closely. 'You made?' she asked the space just above it.

'Uma — Uma did,' Mama said, smiling ingratiatingly.

'Nice,' said Mrs Syal again, 'but my brother, he does not take sweets.'

'No? Oh, take a samosa then, take a

samosa — very spicy,' cried Mama, and handed the plate of samosas to Uma to hand to the young man who sat silently and phlegmatically in a large arm chair at the other end of the room.

Uma gave up wrenching at the ring and did as she was told, and if the samosas slid and slipped all over the plate, at least none landed on the floor. She managed to cross the whole length of the room in her unaccustomed sari and offer him the samosas without an accident. Then all he did was shake his head and refuse them. He had been twisting a handkerchief in his hands throughout the party and Uma could not help noticing how dirty and ragged a piece of cloth it was. It made her look at the owner with a stir of sympathy, but when she did she could not see any sign that it was reciprocated.

The three guests left, climbing into the tonga at the gate, and Mrs Syal told Mama, 'Very nice tea, very nice,' before she left, so that Mama nearly bowed in gratitude. She turned around to her daughters, letting out a long slow exhalation of relief. Now they could wait for the return invitation, she told them. But, unfortunately, none came, and they heard no more from the Syals. The weeks went by with decreasing hope and finally Mama relinquished it altogether, as painfully as Uma had the ring drawn from her finger. 'He must not have liked Uma,' she said bitterly, and it was not clear at whom the bitterness was directed. Then a message was brought them by their neighbour, Mrs Joshi. She pushed her way through the hedge one day, her hair streaming over her shoulders because she had washed it that morning and it was not quite dry. 'I am coming like this only,' she gasped as she climbed the steps to the veranda, placing a hand on each thigh in turn as she climbed them, 'because I must tell you —'

'The Syals sent you?' Mama cried at once, quick to pick up the tone of emergency. 'Uma, go get tea for Aunty,' she hastily ordered.

'No, no tea for me, please — it is my fast day.' Mrs Joshi sank into a basket chair and mopped her face with the end of her sari. Then she looked up, first at Mama and then at Uma. 'How can I tell you? But yesterday Mrs Syal came to see me and — you know what she said?'

'What? What?' Mama cried eagerly, swinging rapidly back and forth on the swing. When Mrs Joshi bit her tongue and held back, she worried, 'She did not like our — ?'

Mrs Joshi touched her ears to show that what she had heard had scandalised her. 'He liked — he liked — but who do you think he liked?' She leant forward and murmured into Mama's ear: 'Aruna. He wanted Mrs Syal to ask for Aruna, not Uma.'

Uma was standing behind the swing, watching and waiting, and Mrs Joshi looked up to see if she had heard. She had not, for all her efforts to do so, but at once Mama gave a scream: 'Aruna? Aruna? He asked for *her?*' and it was no use Mrs Joshi clapping her hand over her mouth and rolling her eyes towards Uma.

Uma gave a startled look and hurried away. Mama did not notice, or care. She was too scandalised, too outraged. 'What? What? He said so? Does he know how old Aruna is? Thirteen! And he dares to ask for the younger daughter when we show him the elder? What kind of family does he think *we* are?'

'Shh, shh,' Mrs Joshi begged her. 'I told them already. I told Mrs Syal —'

But Mama would not be stopped. 'Why did you send these people to us? Such people! You think we would marry our daughter into a family like that? Hah?'

When Uma returned with a tray of glasses of iced water, she found her mother and Mrs

Joshi quarelling so loudly that neither paid any attention to her or the iced water and she set down the tray and went into her room and stayed there all morning, watching Aruna paint her fingernails and then her toenails with a bottle of pink polish. At lunch Mama said nothing of the incident but kept a gloomy silence and threw significant looks at Aruna, partly in accusation and partly in reappraisal.

At thirteen, Aruna still had thin brown legs and wore her hair plaited and tied in loops over her ears with large ribbons. Even though she had to dress in the faded blue cotton slip ordained by the convent, and white not coloured ribbons, there was already something about the way she tossed her head when she saw a man looking at her, with a sidelong look of both scorn and laughter, and the way her foot tapped and her legs changed position, that might have alerted the family to what it could expect. Even if Mama was indignant in refusing, she was impressed too, and — Uma saw — respectful of this display of her younger daughter's power of attraction.

By the time Aruna was fourteen she was rebelling against the blue cotton tunic and the white hair ribbons. At every opportunity

she would shed them and change into flowered silk salwars. 'Silk!' Uma would ex-
claim, and Papa would sit up and take
notice, frowning, but Mama was inclined to
indulge Aruna and perhaps realised, instinctively, that if she did, there would be
rewards to reap. So Aruna fluttered about in
flowered silk, and the hair ribbons were re-
placed with little shiny plastic clips and
clasps, and flowers that she picked from the
dusty shrubs and hedges. When Uma was
still watching to see that Arun did not crawl
off the veranda and break his neck or put
knitting needles or naphthalene balls in his
mouth, Aruna was already climbing into bicycle rickshaws and going off to the cinema
— with girl friends from school, she said.
That was quite true, but she did not mention the young men who took the seats behind them, or even beside them,
tempestuously throwing out a knee, an
elbow, or even a hand at times, and con-
triving to touch the little, flustered, excited
creatures, then followed them home on
their bicycles, weaving through the traffic
and singing ardently along the way.

While Mama searched energetically for a
husband for Uma, families were already
'making enquiries' about Aruna. Yet
nothing could be done about them; it was

imperative that Uma marry first. That was the only decent, the only respectable line of behaviour. That also explained why MamaPapa responded so eagerly to an advertisement in a Sunday newspaper placed by 'a decent family' in search of a bride for their only son. MamaPapa went together to meet them and found it was a cloth merchant's family from the bazaar which had recently begun to prosper and was building a new house on the outskirts of the city. They had purchased a large piece of land in what had formerly been a swamp but was being reclaimed by the municipality by filling it in with city refuse; it was now marked into plots and even had some gates and walls coming up to show the beginnings of urbanisation. The merchant's family had laid the foundation of what would clearly be a palatial dwelling compared to the cramped quarters they had occupied for generations in the city. But, the father explained — disarmingly — they could not proceed until they came into some money, and here the dowry mentioned by Papa would come in useful. He was being frank with Papa, but then it was Papa's daughter who would come to his house as a bride. Papa looked dubious at this confession, but Mama was so delighted by the sight of prospective prosperity that she could not be restrained. They themselves owned no house; Papa had always refused to move out of their rented one with which he was perfectly content, leaving Mama with an enormous, unfulfilled desire for property. Why should Uma not fulfil it if she could not? A negotiated sum was made over as dowry, and the engagement ceremony arranged simultaneously.

Uma was dressed in a new sari of rose-pink organza and was allowed to use lipstick for the first time. Even Aruna was impressed by the results, and hugged Uma spontaneously. The fiancé proved quite presentable, to everyone's surprise. Uma did not exactly speak to him, but they looked at each other and she was able to persuade herself that he was not entirely reprehensible. She wished so much that he was not. When Aruna began on her usual line of fault-finding, Uma interrupted her with a 'Tchh! You're so *critical,* Aruna.'

It was thought that now they were engaged, they might meet a few times — after all, the merchant's family had shown such a desire to leave behind the confines of the bazaar and its old customs and traditions by moving to a brand-new suburb and, with it, a freer way of life — so Mama invited the family over — once, twice, thrice — only to be refused each time. She was puzzled and talked over her apprehensions with Papa who frowned deeply but saw marriage as a women's affair and left it to her. No more was heard from the merchant's family. When they went across to pick a date for the wedding, the merchant was not nearly so expansive and cordial as before. Seated cross-legged on a white sheet on the floor, his forehead freshly smeared with red powder after some religious ceremony he had just attended, he did not seem at all pleased to see them. Quite abruptly, drumming his fingers on his thigh, he informed them that his son had decided to go to Roorkee 'for higher education' and felt he should not be hampered by an early marriage at this stage and had asked for the engagement to be indefinitely postponed. If this did not suit them, they were free to break it off. Mama gasped, pressing her hand to her bosom with pain and horror, while Papa stammered, 'And the dowry? The dowry? What about *that?*' The merchant shifted into a more comfortable position, leaning back against a pile of white bolsters under a framed picture of the goddess Lakshmi and a cloud of incense, and told them that it had been spent on the house. How was he to know his son would change his mind? That was not what he had planned, and he had gone ahead and spent the money on building the house just as he had told MamaPapa he would — had he not? Suddenly he sat up and scowled, haranguing them: had he not? He had gone ahead with preparing a home for their daughter, but fate had willed it otherwise. Could one question fate? Could one? Mama, after a night of frenzied weeping and recrimination, went to Mrs Joshi to tell her how she had been cheated. After listening to her, Mrs Joshi went on calmly chopping betel nuts with her silver scissors, and said, 'If you had come to see me before you went into this, I would have warned you. That Goyal family — everyone knows they have played that trick before. Did they not do the same to the Gunga Mull family? How do you think they bought that land in Khushinagar? And started building such a posh house? The Gunga Mulls too handed over a dowry, and then the engagement was broken off. Such wicked, unscrupulous people — who in this town does not know that?' She gave Mama a severe look. 'You should confide in your friends and neighbours,' she went on steadily, recouping all the ground she had lost through the Syal débâcle. 'We are here to give you help and advice, after all.'

'But I was so happy to find someone for my Uma — after all, her cousin Anamika is already married. I didn't like to wait longer,' Mama sniffed pathetically.

'Yes, that is why the Goyals are able to do such things, because of parents being in too much of a hurry. If parents will not take the time to make proper enquiries, what terrible fates their daughters may have! Be grateful that Uma was not married into a family that could have burnt her to death in order to procure another dowry!'

Leaving Mama to gasp with shock at her terrible words, she stopped chopping betel nuts and called into the garden where Uma was helping Arun balance on a bicycle too big for him, 'Uma, Uma dear, come and sit by your Aunty. You haven't talked to me at all yet. Tell me what you are doing now, dear. Will you come shopping with me for some knitting wool tomorrow?'

Uma, confused by such unexpected attention, stood where she was, not wanting to go near Mama or hear more about the disaster. She pretended Arun's foot was caught in the pedal, and bent over him with solicitude. Mama, who was not in the least fooled, shouted across the row of flower-pots, 'Uma, answer Aunty! She is asking you, don't you hear?'

Eight

Mama gives a start so that the swing jerks under her. 'Aré! Aré!' she screams. 'Uma, look, they are stealing the guavas again. Uma, Uma!'

Uma, indoors, frowns. 'What is it, Mama? I am sleeping, you know.'

'Why are you sleeping? There are thieves in the garden, stealing guavas. Aré!' she screams at the top of her voice.

'Let them steal,' Uma groans, throwing herself about on the bed. The sheets are damp with her perspiration and she feels stifled by them. Eventually she struggles up and goes out to meet the glare on the veranda, blinking. 'Where? Who?'

'There! There! See, they are running away — their hands full of guavas. Where is mali? Call mali. Tell him to guard the garden.'

'He must be asleep, Mama,' Uma says mildly, scratching her head and yawning.

'Everybody is sleeping. Only I stay awake to see what is happening in this house. Thieves attack us — everyone comes and takes what they like because you are all sleeping.'

'It is so hot, Mama,' Uma protests, and trails listlessly back to her bed where she sits on the edge, yawning, plaiting her hair and listening to Mama grumbling outside.

∽

There were so many marriage proposals for Aruna that Uma's unmarried state was not only an embarrassment but an obstruction. Here was Aruna visibly ripening on the branch, asking to be plucked: no one had to teach her how to make samosas or help her to dress for an occasion. Instinctively, she knew. The pale, pale pink sari, the slender chain of seed pearls, the fresh flowers, the demure downcast turn of the eyes, the little foot in the red slipper thrusting out suddenly like a tongue, and the laughter low and sly. Mama watched and wondered, Papa humphed and hawed and scowled but Uma could see it was a façade and concealed a pleasure he would not allow himself to express. Sometimes there was something in his look that he did not quite control and gave him away, and that upset Mama and made her speak sharply and severely. Then he looked a bit confused, and withdrew. Uma did not know what was expected of her in this situation; she waited patiently to be disposed.

When Aruna said to her, laughing, 'Uma, why don't you cut your hair short? Like Lila Aunty? It will suit you, you know,' she retorted 'Tchh! What silly ideas you have,' and was not only annoyed but hurt as well: she had caught the mockery in Aruna's tone. When they were younger, and Uma had brought back those report cards from school filled with red Fs, Aruna had watched in silence while Papa thundered and Mama complained, and waited for a decent interval before proffering her own report card, satisfyingly blue and green, and collected their praise. When the first two attempts at marrying Uma off had ended in disgrace, she had listened to Mama's storms of temper, saying, 'I told you he was no good, didn't I?' and looked sympathetically at Uma. But now a certain mockery was creeping into her behaviour, a kind of goading, like that a sprightly little dog will subject a large dull ox to when it wants a little action. Uma's ears were already filled to saturation with Mama's laments, and Aruna's little yelps of laughter were additional barbs. Had anyone looked, they might have noticed that Uma's face was losing its childish openness of expression and taking on a look of continual care. Arun, who did not really understand what was happening, and was no part of it, seemed to sense this change: he stopped teasing her so much, appealed to her more as an adult now, then became impatient because she could not help him with his multiplication and division exercises, or throw a ball so he might practise his batting. She missed his teasing, and she missed Aruna's sympathy and solidarity too. The tightly knit fabric of family that had seemed so stifling and confining now revealed holes and gaps that were frightening — perhaps the fabric would not hold, perhaps it would not protect after all. There was cousin Anamika's example, the one no one wanted to see: but how could one not?

Mama worked hard at trying to dispose of Uma, sent her photograph around to everyone who advertised in the matrimonial columns of the Sunday papers, but it was always returned with the comment 'We are looking for someone taller/ fairer/ more educated, for Sanju/Pinku/Dimpu', even though the photograph had been carefully touched up by the local photographer, giving Uma pink checks and almost-blue eyes as she perched on a velvet stool before a cardboard balustrade in his studio.

The man who finally approved of it and considered it good enough for him was not so young; 'he was married before,' his relatives wrote candidly, 'but he has no issue.' He was 'in the pharmaceutical business, earning decent income', which was taken to mean that he was a travelling salesman who received a commission in addition to his salary. 'He is a good family man with sense of responsibility,' they wrote, which was interpreted to mean he was living with his parents in an extended family. Since it was clear Uma was not going to receive any other offer no matter what a good job the photographer had done with his unpromising material, Mama and Papa decided to proceed with the negotiations. The dowry offered by Papa, although modest since he had already thrown one away — as he never stopped reminding the women in the family — must have seemed like a bonus to a man who may not have expected more than one dowry in a lifetime. It was accepted with alacrity.

Since the previous meeting between the

prospective bride and groom had proved so unpropitious, it was tacitly decided to do without one in this case. And so the bridegroom's party was on its way. Mama frantically supervised the cooking of meals and making of sweets for three days in a row. Papa was seeing to the marquee being set up on the lawn, the priest and all his requirements in the way of ceremony and ritual, and the musicians to play during the reception. Uma found herself richer by a dozen saris, a set of gold jewellery and another of pearls, then was handed a garland and posted at the entrance to the marquee to wait for the bridegroom.

He came from his town by train along with his brothers, cousins, father and other male relatives as well as a party of male friends. At the railway station they got into taxis and auto rickshaws and arrived at the head of the street where they were met by a brass band and the horse they had hired, a rather spindly and knock-kneed one but brightly dressed in garlands and tinsel. This he mounted, with help from his brothers and friends, and so proceeded to their gate, his friends dancing and turning somersaults the whole length of the street while the band played 'Colonel Bogey'.

Uma felt the drum and the trumpet sound

in the very depths of her chest, pounding on it as if it were a tin pan. Her henna-painted hands, holding the garland, trembled. Mama stood behind her, securing the jasmines in her hair, and Aruna danced from one foot to the other, her lips stained red with the lipstick she had been allowed to use at last, and cried, 'Uma, he is coming! He is coming!'

He slid off the horse, making it crash its knees together and nearly fall, then approached Uma with a damp and wilting garland. His hands, too, shook a little. His brothers, who supported him on each side, steered him towards Uma, then raised the curtain of silver and gold tinsel from his face. He looked at Uma glumly and without much interest. What he saw did not seem to make him change his attitude. He handed over his garland and Uma was made to drape hers over his head. She bit her lips as she did so, he seemed so reluctant to accept it. The man looked as old to her as Papa, nearly, and was grossly overweight too, while his face was pockmarked. None of this disturbed her as much, however, as did his sullen expression. He so resembled all the other men who had ever looked her way — they had all been reduced to precisely this state of unenthusiasm — that she relinquished all her foolishly unrealistic hopes.

So it was in this spirit that they sat through the long ceremony; afterwards Uma remembered only that the smoke from the ceremonial fire over which the priest presided blew into her face all the way through it (and ayah, who squatted on her haunches nearby in the new sari given for the occasion, whispered in her ear, 'That means he will follow you everywhere,' and tinkled her many new glass bangles gaily by clapping her hands at her own wit). Every now and then Mama nudged her and that was a signal for her to throw rice, or oil, into the fire at which the priest cried loudly, 'Om swa-ha! Om swa-ha!' after which he dropped his voice to a mutter again while running through the interminable Sanskrit verses audible and comprehensible to him alone. Not that anyone was listening, apart from Uma and her husband who had no choice. All the guests and the family wandered around the marquee, drinking soft drinks and shouting with laughter. Occasionally one of them would come by and sit for a while to watch by her side. Uma caught a glimpse now and then of Bakul Uncle and Lila Aunty, Mrs Joshi, the others. She watched to see if Ramu would appear, but he did not — he was on his farm, his parents said (they had bought it for him in a plan to keep him from drink — or drugs, whatever it was) and no one knew if he had received the invitation; he had become very uncommunicative, they said. And Anamika — Anamika was with her husband and in-laws, they had not given her permission to come. 'They just can't let her out of their sight for even one day, they love her so much,' Lila Aunty assured them.

The ceremony wound on at its own ponderous pace. Finally the sullen bridegroom broke in and said curtly to the priest, 'Cut it short, will you — that's enough now.' The priest looked offended, Uma was mortified. If he could not even tolerate the wedding ceremony, how would he tolerate their marriage?

When it was over, her husband took her to the railway station — not on his horse, Uma was relieved to find, but in a car hired for the occasion. All his relatives were already on the platform with the luggage, carrying the presents of boxes of sweets that Mama had given them, discussing the wedding — and particularly the wedding feast that had followed — in loud voices; Uma gathered they had considerable complaints to make about it. She was heaved into a four-berth compartment with him, his elder brother and sister-in-law. None of them paid her any attention once they had found her a place to sit on the bunk. They pulled out a pack of cards, sat themselves cross-legged on the next bunk and began to play rummy.

The train clattered through the dusty night, stopping frequently at stations that were luridly lit with naphtha flares and swarming with tea and peanut vendors, then rattled on. Uma tried to sit upright and stay awake, but the exhaustion of the entire day and the rocking motion of the train made her sag, then collapse on her side and fall asleep with her cheek and her flower garlands pressed into the grimy green rexine of the bunk. She woke once in the dark, with only the blue night light gloomily lit above, and found herself pressed against the wall by a heavy figure dressed in slippery nylon garments and many bangles: it was her sister-in-law, rhythmically snoring. She raised her head in a panic to see where her husband was — she knew she must stay with him, Mama had said so — and saw mounds of flesh heaped on other bunks; he was one of them, she told herself, and tried to go back to sleep, suffocated as she was by her sister-in-law's thick fleshy back and odour of perspiration.

At daybreak they arrived at a small but

crowded and clamorous station in the town where Uma now was to live. The marriage party climbed down from the train, yawning and unwashed, looking much the worse for wear. They got into tongas tiredly and crossly and made their way through bazaars full of bicycle rickshaws and barrows to their family home, a low yellow house in a lane where cows munched garbage and dogs slunk about, growling. Here Uma was handed over to her husband's female relatives — a hardbitten mother who kept her teeth tightly clenched on a betel nut as she examined Uma with shrewd small eyes, and the wives of his brothers, and their children. Having shown Uma into a room that led off the kitchen, and put down the trunk that held her clothes — those containing the things Mama had bought for the house were to follow — her husband muttered, 'You may rest. I am going to work.'

'To work?' Uma asked in surprise, for the wedding had surely been an unusual event, a kind of holiday, and she had not expected it to end quite so abruptly.

He nodded and mumbled something like, 'In Meerut,' and disappeared.

Uma sat down on the bed. It was a string bed with the bedding rolled up at one end. There was nowhere else to sit. There was a string across the room on which a few clothes were hung — men's clothes, her husband's clothes, she thought, quickly averting her eyes from the pyjamas and striped drawers. But there was nothing else to look at.

After a few minutes the women started appearing — first one sister, then another, then the children, finally the mother. They stood in a ring around her, staring. They spoke to each other, making remarks about her complexion, her hair, her jewellery, her sari, the size of her hands and feet. Some lifted her hand and examined the ring, the bangles, the henna pattern. Then one sister marched to the trunk. 'Open it,' she said. Uma got up and knelt beside it to unlock it. She found her hands shaking again. They came up close, pressing against her, in order to reach into the trunk and go through its contents. They addressed each other only, making comments on her saris, her jewellery, the bottle of Evening in Paris perfume Aruna had given her, but saying nothing to her. Then they withdrew to the kitchen, one after the other, and the last one looked back over her shoulder and said, 'Change your clothes and come — we have to prepare food now.'

Uma did as she was told, uncomfortably

aware as she undressed and dressed, of their presence on the other side of the door which she had not the courage to lock and bolt. Dressed in one of her new cotton saris, she went out to the kitchen to join them, hoping they would speak directly to her, ask questions of her and so begin some communication at last. But although they gave her instructions about what to do — slice the onions and peel vegetables, pick the dhal clean and wash the rice, which she did clumsily and awkwardly because she was not used to squatting on the floor to work and had not much experience with such work anyway — they continued to talk to each other, in lowered voices, but still loud enough for her to hear their remarks on her clumsiness, her awkwardness, her clothes and her looks. She gathered they were not impressed by her and worked with her face sunk into her cotton sari and her ears burning.

When the men returned from work, they too gave Uma a silent scrutiny as they settled down to eat. Uma was surprised that Harish was not amongst them. She did not dare ask them where he was for fear of not getting an answer. After helping the women wash the pots and pans under a splashing tap in the corner, and soaked through by the exercise, she went to her room, thinking he might come late, he was working extra hours to make up for his time away at the wedding. She lay awake on the string cot the whole night, listening to the kitchen tap drip — it was tied up with a rag and water ran from it constantly — and the stray dog in the lane outside whine, coughing and talk in the other rooms, and then, when at last it was grey with dawn and he had still not come, she got up and went into the kitchen in an anxiety that was like a choking of her throat, wanting to ask for news of him.

His mother was making tea in a great pan, boiling milk and tea leaves and sugar together. 'Did he not tell you, he has gone to Meerut?' she asked crisply and, Uma thought, contemptuously.

For several weeks, Uma kept writing home to tell the family that Harish was away in Meerut on work and had not returned. In those weeks she learnt how to cut vegetables in pieces of exactly the same size, how to grind spices into a wet paste and how to tell one dhal from another. All the speech directed at her was in the form of instructions; there was no other.

Then one day Papa arrived at the house. Uma's mouth fell open with shock and alarm when she saw him storming in at the door, and hurried towards him, afraid that he had brought bad news. It was bad, but it was not anything she had expected: Papa had learnt that they had been duped. Harish was married already, had a wife and four children in Meerut where he ran an ailing pharmaceutical factory to save which he had needed another dowry which had led him to marry again.

The scene that followed was surely a unique and memorable one but Uma's response to it was to shut not only her eyes and ears to it — she had gone into her room, shut the door and sat on the bed, wrapping her sari over her head, around her ears and mouth and eyes, till it was all over — but even her mind, so as to block out a memory she could not have lived with. It consisted of Papa raving and ranting at one end, the mother-in-law screaming and screeching at the other, the brothers shouting and threatening in between, and the sisters-in-law clustering together to watch all the parties in a kind of bitter satisfaction.

So Uma went home with Papa. By doing the same journey on a day train, it was as if the entire process was being reversed. The compartment was crowded this time with strangers, but Papa had so lost control of

himself, was so beside himself, as not to be-
have normally or sanely: he beat his head
with his fists, and moaned aloud about the
dowry and the wedding expenses while everyone, all of them strangers — women with
babies and baskets of food, men reading papers or playing cards or discussing business
— turned to listen with the keenest of interest, throwing significant looks at Uma
who kept her head wrapped up in her sari in
an effort to screen her shame. By the time
they reached their own station, everyone
along the way knew of her humiliation and
her ruin. It was fortunate that none of them
were the lawyers and magistrates Papa ordinarily met: he would not have cared so to
lose control of himself and betray his gull-
ibility before them. It was necessary to get
himself under control by the time he returned to his own circle and his normal
round. Stepping out at the station that
looked so large, so orderly and civilised by
comparison with the others they had passed
— electric fans hung from the high ceiling,
magazines and paperbacks were arrayed on
the shelves of Wheeler's stall — he fell silent
and resumed his ordinarily grim appearance. Uma was relieved; the disintegration
of Papa's personality had pained her as
much as that of her marriage.

At home Mama opened every one of the trunks Papa had insisted Uma pack and bring with her, and checked every item in them. Papa had managed to retrieve her jewellery by threatening the family with legal action — oh, what a mistake they had made by choosing a bride from a legal family, an educated family! — but it had been too demeaning to fight for every pot and pan they had contributed to the kitchen, and there was a great deal, Mama lamented, that was lost. While these scenes were being played out in the centre, the heart of the family and household, Arun withdrew to its outermost limits, hiding in his room under a blanket of comic books. If anyone were to look in, Arun was not to be found; in his place were Captain Marvel, Superman and Phantom.

At night, in the dark and the silence, Aruna whispered to her sister, 'Uma. Uma. Did — did he touch you, Uma?' making Uma bury her head in her pillow and howl 'No! No!' so that Aruna fell back with a little sigh of disappointment. Next day she reported it to ayah who reported it to Mama. Mama and ayah appeared relieved, as if a great weight had been lifted from them.

The marriage was somehow cancelled, annulled. Uma was never told of the legal proceedings involved. It was assumed she would not understand, and was never quite certain if she had never actually married or if she was now divorced. Divorced — what a scandalous ring to the word! She could hardly bring herself to pronounce it, she knew no one who was. Once when she asked Mama — hesitantly, out of a curiosity she could not restrain — Mama smacked at the air as if at a mosquito, and snapped, 'Don't talk about it! Don't remind me of it!'

Having cost her parents two dowries, without a marriage to show in return, Uma was considered ill-fated by all and no more attempts were made to marry her off.

Once Uma overheard Mama telling Mira-masi, who was visiting, 'All those astrologers we consulted about her horoscope, what liars they proved to be,' only to have Mira-masi reply, 'It was not to astrologers you should have taken her, but to the Lord Shiva, to pray for His blessing instead.' 'And you think your Lord Shiva would have blessed *her?*' Mama cried. Mira-masi gave her a severe look, and Uma heard her say in her most dignified manner, 'She *is* blessed by the Lord. The Lord has rejected the men you chose for her because He has chosen her for Himself.'

Uma, thunderstruck, crept away in the dark of the shadows flung by the neem tree across the terrace where they sat talking, after Papa had gone to bed (Papa did not tolerate such talk). The thought that the Lord Shiva was pursuing her made her no more comfortable than the thought of all the men who had fled from her. The Lord Shiva may have been an acceptable husband to Mira-masi but even He, at least in the form of the brass image that had been stolen from her, had proved Himself elusive. She wanted to point this out to Mira-masi and Mama, to say, 'You see? It is not so easy,' but the two women sat silently beside each other, darkly brooding, and Uma knew, seeing them, their grim presences throwing dark shadows upon the wall, that she had not had their experiences, that hers was other: that of an outcast from the world of marriage, the world which, all the murmuring and whispering and muttering implied, was all that mattered.

Retreating to her room, she sank down on the floor, against the wall, and put her arms around her knees and wondered what it would have been like to have the Lord Shiva for a husband, have Him put His arms around her. 'Did he touch you?'

Aruna had wanted to know. No, he had not, and sitting there in the dark, Uma tried to imagine what it would have been like if he had.

Nine

Uma is alone. MamaPapa have gone to the club to play bridge. Uma has her supper on a tray; the cook has gone home early and left it for her on the veranda table. After she has eaten it, she goes to her room. She looks around for something to do that she cannot do when MamaPapa are at home, needing her every minute as they do. She opens her cupboard, humming to herself musingly as she runs her eyes over her folded saris, her boxes full of matching bangles, the lace-edged handkerchiefs. Of course she knows what she wants to do: she reaches to the top for a shoebox full of old Christmas cards. Over the years, the collection has grown to a sizeable one. She carries it across to her bed and sits there cross-legged, looking through them — the cards collected for her by Mrs

O'Henry, the Baptist missionary's wife, by Mother Agnes, and friends and neighbours. She runs her finger along the gilt crosses and embossed poinsettias, she plays with fragments of ribbon and lace, and reads through the merry little jingles that make her smile: they are so loving and bright with goodwill and friendship. She binds them all up again with string and stows them away like treasure — to her they are treasure. If anyone were to touch them, their magic would be somehow defaced: that is how she feels about them.

She wanders through the house which is shadowy, a bit sinister; when MamaPapa are out, all the lights are switched off save one, of very low voltage, to save electricity, and there is only just enough light to allow Uma to make her way past the heavy, dark pieces of furniture. She stops at a three-legged table on which the telephone stands. She lifts the ear phone, taps at it, humming. Then her fingers fit into the openings for the numbers and she is dialling. The phone rings in some other dark, shadowy house. She bites her lip at her own audacity and stealth. This is not something she can do when MamaPapa are present: their avid curiosity and their disapproval would prevent her.

At last the ringing of the phone is answered. Uma's face falls: it is the servant who has answered. 'O'Henry memsahib, is she in?' Uma finds herself enquiring. She fears Papa might spring out of the shadows and grasp her by the shoulder and demand an explanation for her deceit, or payment for the call. To risk so much just to hear the servant boy's sleepy, sulky voice saying no, she is not. 'Where has she gone?' Uma cries, and bangs the phone down. The furniture looms up around her, threateningly. She pushes past it and goes out on the veranda.

At least the air is clearer here and has something free about it, still as it is. Over the top of the dusty trees, there is a new moon to be seen, very pale and far away. The jasmine bush at the foot of the stairs is in full bloom, releasing its perfume in white clouds in the dark. She plucks one and, with it on the palm of her hand, goes across to the swing and sits there. She gives herself a little push with her foot and sets it in motion. She hums a tune from a film she was once taken to see by the neighbours. 'Sweet, sweet moonlight,' she sings as she had seen the heroine do, in a garden garishly lit by an electric moon and with paper roses tumbling down from a cardboard trellis. 'Pale pale moonlight,' she sings to the flower in the cup of her hand.

146

Then the headlights of the car appear at the gate, two probing white eyes: MamaPapa are back. Abruptly, Uma gets up from the swing and goes into her room. When they come up the stairs to the veranda, the swing still rocks, creaking back and forth as if a ghost has sat on it.

Mama goes and bangs upon Uma's door. 'Uma, Uma, we're back.'

Uma stands on the other side, holding the white flower. She bites her lip and does not answer.

Mama bangs and rattles for a while, then stops. Uma hears her go off to her own room, grumbling, 'Already sleeping, always sleeping. . . .'

No one was at all surprised but everyone was gratified when Aruna brought off the marriage that Uma had dismally failed to make. As was to be expected, she took her time, showed a reluctance to decide, played choosy, but soon enough made the wisest, most expedient choice — the handsomest, the richest, the most exciting of the suitors who presented themselves. So exciting were his dark, saturnine looks, the curl of his lips and the way his sideburns grew right down to the line of his jaw, and so lavish the future predicted for him, that MamaPapa were actually a little perturbed. Prudently, they wished for someone a little less handsome, a little less showy (*they* were neither, after all), and bade caution, suggested waiting to see who else might turn up. But when Aruna had made up her mind, then no one could stop her, and she had her way.

The wedding was a splendid one — not like Uma's drab, cut-rate affair. At Aruna's insistence, the reception was held in the lobby of the Carlton Hotel. Instead of a brass band from the bazaar, she had Tiny Lopez's band play dance music. What was more, she persuaded Papa to throw what she called a cocktail party to welcome Arvind and his family the day before the wedding. This was to be an event so chic — and untraditional — as had never been witnessed before in the town, at least by their relatives. Unfortunately, Uma spoilt it considerably by her appalling tendency, developed — they were all certain — during her stay at the ashram with Mira-masi, of throwing 'fits'. The guests were milling around in the most elegant chiffon saris and sherwanis, the air was thick with the fumes of tuberoses and whisky, when Uma, who had been sent to fetch a fresh trayload of party snacks, instead stood rigid with the empty tray in her hands, staring ahead of her. When Mama gave her a little nudge to rouse her and hurry her, she simply keeled over as if she had been cut down with an axe. She fell heavily at the guests' feet, managing to strike her head against the tin tray so that it was cut open dramatically, and when they ran to help her up, she began to roll on the ground, just as she had done at the ashram, her eyes fixed, her teeth clenched, jerking her shoulders and drumming her heels uncontrollably. That is what they told her she did — till Dr Dutt was fetched from the other end of the marquee and came at once, thrust a handkerchief into Uma's mouth to prevent her from biting her tongue, washed her face with a glass of cold water, and then had her carried to her bedroom, all so quickly and efficiently that not everyone in the marquee even became aware of the incident.

Uma, sitting up in bed that night, tried to picture the appalling scene that she could not at all remember. She listened to Aruna's voice lashing at her, flailing her with accusations. She had spoilt the party, the cocktail party. What would Arvind's family think of them, of Aruna who had a sister who was an idiot, an hysteric? She should be put away, locked up, Aruna sobbed. 'I should be locked up,' Uma moaned, along with her. 'Lock me up, Mama, lock me up!' They howled together till Mama came marching in. 'What is going on here? Go to sleep, Aruna. Be quiet, Uma. I don't want to hear another word. Tomorrow is the wedding day and I've had enough trouble already. Now be quiet and go to sleep, you two.' Uma lay down obediently but could not hold back another moan: 'Oh, Mama, please!' while Aruna hissed one last threat, 'Don't you *dare* do that at the wedding, don't you *dare!*'

Uma did not, and the wedding was as chic as Aruna had planned it; the ceremony itself brief, its chief features being Aruna's elaborate sari and jewellery and the groom's maharaja-style turban. Bakul Uncle and Lila Aunty approved, although Lila Aunty sighed, 'If only Anamika could be here, but that family just want her with them all the time,' and sighed again. No one mentioned Ramu; he was not considered fit for society any more and had not been sent an invitation.

The Carlton Hotel provided the dinner, and even if some relatives refused to touch food cooked by who knew what low-caste cooks in what polluted kitchens, most of the guests were profoundly impressed and grateful and said so in heartfelt tones as they left, compensating Papa somewhat for the shocking expense. Only Dr Dutt had nothing to say to the parents except, 'And how is dear Uma? I'm glad to see she is looking a little better today but I think she needs a tonic,' but then Dr Dutt was known for her abrupt ways and was excused because she was a doctor.

And Aruna was whisked away to a life that she had said would be 'fantastic' and was. Arvind had a job in Bombay and bought a flat in a housing block in Juhu, facing the beach, and Aruna said it was 'like a dream'. These were the words that Aruna used in her letters. They were not words anyone in their town used, either because they did not know them or because nothing in their town merited them. But such words, such use of them did seem to raise Aruna to another level — distant and airy as Uma imagined must be her flat overlooking the sea. She wondered if she would ever see it, but Aruna was so busy either visiting Arvind's family in Ahmedabad or having them visit her in Bombay that there never seemed a time when she could have Uma and MamaPapa to stay, or even just Uma by herself. She did visit them from time to time — she even returned there to have her first child as custom dictated, but the second child was born in a modern nursing home in Bombay because Aruna could not bear to repeat that experience. Mama begged Papa to write and ask her to bring the children on visits, but perhaps Papa's clipped, official style of correspondence did not convey sufficient family feeling, and Aruna came only at long intervals so that every time they saw the children, they had turned into strangers again and were unrecognisable.

The earlier visits quite terrified Uma because she was sure she could not handle such small and precious infants while Aruna handed them over quite matter-of-factly, clearly expecting her, as the maiden aunt, to do so. Had she not helped to bring up Arun? Yes, but Uma could not explain how it was different to care for someone in one's own family and why it was altogether different to be handed Aruna's babies in their expensive and unsuitable clothing and expected to feed them their strange 'formula'. When Aruna casually asked her to bathe them, she did not dare place them in the basin of water provided, she was so sure she would let them slip out of her fingers and drown. So she just wiped them with a damp towel and handed them back, pretending they were bathed. Aruna did not notice. She was out most of the time, visiting her girl friends, showing them her Bombay acquisitions.

On one of these visits home, Uma walked into her room to find Aruna sitting in front of the mirror and applying her make-up. She came over to watch and Aruna showed her: 'See, this is for the eyelids, and this for the eyelashes, and here is something for outlining the eyes. Then for the cheeks — first this cream, then this lotion, finally the powder and just the lightest, lightest touch of rouge — this one, or perhaps that one —' Uma had a pile of washed, folded nappies in her arms; she watched for a while, grew impatient and said, 'So that's what you've got all over your face. We were wondering.'

Aruna slammed her make-up kit shut. 'Yes, this is what women in Bombay use. They don't walk around looking like washerwomen unless they *are* washerwomen,' she told Uma. 'Now *you* sit on the stool, here, and let me try and do something about you. Why do you still wear your hair in a pigtail, like a schoolgirl? Let me cut it for you —'

Uma gave a shriek and ran giggling to the door. 'Cut my hair? You can't! Mama will kill me —'

'Mama won't kill you! I cut my hair and here I am.'

Uma had fled, holding onto her pigtail and dropping nappies all along the way. The thought of having her hair cut, like a film actress, made her giggle. But later she teased Mama, 'What if I cut off my hair, like Aruna?'

'Cut it off? You want to look like a —' Mama wouldn't say the word, preferring to just suggest it. 'You want the neighbours to say you've become a —'

Aruna gave an angry snort and walked off, saying, 'You people are villagers!'

Uma quickly grabbed the advantage of the moment. 'She wanted to cut it off,' she confided slyly. 'She's picked up all these ideas in Bombay. She may even try to make *you* cut off your hair, Mama!'

Mama and Uma collapsed against each other on the swing, giggling.

When her daughter was a little older, Aruna could use her new expertise on the child, curling her hair and designing her frocks. Aisha looked like a doll, but was given to frightful temper tantrums and would throw things at the wall and kick and scream with rage if anyone suggested she drink her milk or go and wash her hands.

Mama and Uma were awed by the amount of temper the small thing could contain and release, but when she was through with it, she would become quite docile and sit on Uma's bed, going through her box of bangles or the Christmas cards — although Uma could not help hovering nervously over her while she did so, not sure when she might decide to tear one up or throw all of them away.

It was Dinesh who was more worrying, although, on the surface, much more tractable. He spent most of his time sitting with his schoolboy uncle Arun's collection of American comic books and reading them with his mouth open and his hair falling into his eyes. He would stir and show signs of life only when he had gone through the whole collection and there was not one left to read. Then he had to be taken to the bazaar so he could buy some more. Arun would come home from school and angrily bundle up his comics and put them out of reach.

The air gun was another matter. Papa had bought it for Arun, who never used it, and Dinesh found it behind a heap of old shoes in the cupboard, and was greatly intrigued. Arun flatly refused to show him how to use it but, one afternoon, Uma was woken out of her sleep by some sharp cracking, splitting sounds in the next room, and got up to see what it was. She found Dinesh standing there with the air gun in his hand, looking down at a pigeon he had shot off the skylight ledge and which now lay dying in a tumult of bloodied feathers on the floor. It was not wounded badly enough to die and made helpless efforts to bring its wings together and rise to its feet. The way the beak hung open and the eyes bulged, however, did not seem hopeful signs, and it tottered around blindly. Uma cried to Dinesh, 'Shoot it, quick! Kill it, please!' Dinesh was watching it with a curious expression on his flushed face; he put out his tongue and licked his lip, then grinned at her, a little frightenedly. Uma continued to scream at him till at last he did what he was told. Then he enjoyed telling his furious mother and his appalled grandmother that it was Uma who made him kill it. 'She told me to shoot it,' he kept repeating with pleasure, seeing it made her face pale with anger each time.

Uma did not look forward to his next visit but he proved less offensive when he came again, perhaps because he hardly stayed at home. She noticed he was always slipping off in a furtive manner through the guava trees and the gap in the hedge, to the neighbours'. There was no cause for concern in this except there were no children of his age in that household and there was no knowing what the attraction was. Tactful enquiries brought forth a blank look on Mrs Joshi's face since she had not seen Dinesh around.

Then Uma glimpsed him, through the dusty guava tree foliage, and the pale, twisted branches, with the driver's young son, behind the neighbours' garage. She peered and peered from the edge of the veranda but was too shortsighted to see what they were up to. Another time she saw Dinesh balanced on the crossbar of a bicycle ridden by the boy, going round in narrow circles, both boys leaning into each other's arms and laughing hilariously. It seemed innocuous enough but Dinesh was old enough to ride the bicycle himself and did not need to be driven around.

That evening on the veranda, Uma mentioned Panna, the driver's son, to him, and Dinesh looked at her out of the corner of his eyes, then ruffled his hair so it came down over his forehead. Papa scowled: he had never allowed his children to play with the servants' children, it was a rule of his, and Arun had never played with Panna. Seeing that, Dinesh shuffled his feet on the floor and made off. No one said anything more and Dinesh continued to spend his time in

Panna's company, but always out of sight. If anyone did catch a glimpse of them, they looked up with bland, practised looks of innocence followed by sharp bursts of laughter when left to themselves. Mama did not urge Dinesh to come again.

Once there was a chance Uma would visit Aruna in Bombay. At least, her optician, on giving her a check-up, said quite solemnly, 'There is something there that needs more testing. I can't do it here' — he gestured to his little clinic in the bazaar, patients crowded upon the benches along the walls, stray dogs and vendors pressing in at the door — 'you really need to consult a specialist. See if you can visit one in Bombay.' Uma flushed hectically at the thought and hurried home to give the news to Papa. Papa's brow blackened visibly and he sank into a morose heap on the swing, and had to be reminded by Mama of Uma's news. 'Harumph,' he said, choking. 'Harumph. No need, no need. Why waste money on a trip to Bombay? Our optician is good enough, good enough. No need to go to Bombay, no need at all. Harumph.'

Then Aruna brought along her mother-in-law and other relatives of Arvind's who wanted to bathe in the holy river. It was a fraught visit, Aruna frantic that Mama and Uma spruce up the crumbling old house and make it presentable, and acquit themselves well as hosts and her family. She spent the entire visit hissing under her breath at Uma, 'Can't you bring out a *clean* tablecloth? Don't you see this one is all stained?' or following Mama to her dressing room to complain, 'Why have you washed your hair in the middle of the morning? Couldn't you do it at night instead of sitting here with it all open? It looks so *sloppy!*' or dashing into the kitchen to show the cook how to make a salad — 'All he does is slice up tomatoes and cucumbers and onions and spread them flat on the plate — where's the *dressing?*' As for Arun, she took one horrified look at him, at his drooping khaki shorts, his unlaced gym shoes, his uncombed hair falling over his forehead, and gave up, with a dramatic rolling of her eyes; she could not believe he existed, as he did, and preferred to act as if he did not (which suited him very well). Even Papa, not easily shaken in his profound conviction of his status and authority, seemed uneasy and sat upright and tried to converse instead of scowling into space as was his habit and one from which no one in the family had ever tried to pry him loose (being even more afraid of his words than his silence). Aruna scolded him, 'Don't you ever get the house painted, Papa? Look how the walls are peeling. It's just falling *down*,' and, 'What happened to the driver's uniform? He used to wear one, where is it?' If MamaPapa had once had qualms about her marrying into a family she could not keep up with they need not have worried — every trace of her provincial roots was obliterated and overlaid by the bright sheen of the metropolis. It was they who could not keep up.

The only thing that made them tolerate her behaviour was the evidence that she directed it not only towards them but even at her husband Arvind, who came to deposit his family there and would collect them later. Mama was astonished at the way Aruna scolded him continuously. 'Oh, you have again spilt tea in your saucer. Now it will drip all over you,' she would cry, or pull at his shirt and say, 'But this shirt does not go with those trousers. Why didn't you ask me first?' Clearly Aruna had a vision of a perfect world in which all of them — her own family as well as Arvind's — were flaws she was constantly uncovering and correcting in her quest for perfection. It made for a very uncomfortable household but it

160

was, in a way, touching. Seeing Aruna vexed to the point of tears because the cook's pudding had sunk and spread instead of remaining upright and solid, or because Arvind had come to dinner in his bedroom slippers, or Papa was wearing a t-shirt with a hole under one arm, Uma felt pity for her: was this the realm of ease and comfort for which Aruna had always pined and that some might say she had attained? Certainly it brought her no pleasure: there was always a crease of discontent between her eyebrows and an agitation that made her eyelids flutter, disturbing Uma who noticed it.

Once even Mama asked if she had something in her eye to make her blink so, and when Aruna angrily denied this, Mama told her about the optician's suggestion that Uma have her eyes examined by a specialist in Bombay. 'A specialist — in Bombay!' Aruna gave a shriek. 'Do you know what that would *cost?*' She seemed so horrified by the idea that Uma felt bound to reassure her and say she was sure Dr Tandon was really quite good enough. 'Of course he is!' Aruna exclaimed.

All that Uma enjoyed of that visit was the trip on the river in the big flat-bottomed boat they hired to hold all the guests who had come to take the ritual bath. Uma was excited — Mama had never permitted her family this dangerous rite; she saw no reason why one should place one's life in danger to prove one's religious belief which could surely be taken for granted.

The boatman poled the boat slowly to where two rivers met, throwing up a sandbar where the water ran shallow in the very centre of the great green depths. He steadied the boat by plunging the pole deep into the rippled sand and advised them to bathe at this point, cautioning them against stepping off the bar and against currents.

Everyone was in a state of high excitement, all the women in light cotton saris worn specially for the occasion, now clambering over the side, screaming when the boat rocked and clutching each other in pleasurable panic. Uma, thrilled by this license, simply sprang off the prow and plunged in without hesitation, as if this were what she had been preparing to do all her life. Immediately she disappeared into the water, having leapt not onto the sandbar where the others stood splashing but into the deep dark river itself. She went down like a stone while the women screamed, 'Uma, Uma! Where is she?' Someone caught at the end of her sari as it floated by, a scrap of white muslin, then the arm that it enfolded, and the shoulder, and hauled her out onto the sandbar. She knelt there, in the shallows, water pouring from her mouth and hair. She rose, gasping for breath, struggling, flailing her arms and choking like a big, wounded water bird. Aruna's voice called out in warning, 'Uma, don't! Don't you dare, Uma —' and Uma shook herself and wrapped her arms about her and blinked the water out of her eyes and stared back at her. No, she was not going to have a fit, she assured Aruna with a pleading, pacifying look; this was not a fit, she promised.

What it was was that when she had plunged into the dark water and let it close quickly and tightly over her, the flow of the river, the current, drew her along, clasping her and dragging her with it. It was not fear she felt, or danger. Or, rather, these were only what edged something much darker, wilder, more thrilling, a kind of exultation — it was exactly what she had always wanted, she realised. Then they had saved her. The saving was what made her shudder and cry, there on the sandbar, soaking wet, while the morning sun leapt up in the hazy, sand-coloured sky and struck the boat, the brass pots that the women held, and their white drifting garments in the water.

Ten

Mrs O'Henry is giving a coffee party. She has
invited Uma. Uma is flushed with delight, the
bottle-thick lenses of her spectacles gleam
with pleasure as she listens to the voice on the
telephone, that deep, sing-song burr.
MamaPapa, watching her intently from the
swing, purse their lips.

'Who was that?' they ask, although they
have already guessed.

'Mrs O'Henry — she has invited me to a
coffee party.' Uma can hardly speak; she
would like to keep this treasured invitation
to herself — it is for herself alone, after all —
and would have preferred not to divulge it.
Of course that is out of the question.

'Why?' asks Papa.

'Coffee? Why coffee?' asks Mama.

Uma jerks her head back. 'Why?' she

snaps back at them. 'She is giving a party — a coffee party, not a tea party — and she has invited some ladies, and me.'

'Tchch!' Mama pronounces her opinion of this ridiculous, outlandish invention, and moodily swings back and forth.

'Why? What is wrong?' Uma demands heatedly.

'Nothing is wrong,' Mama replies sourly, 'only I don't see the need for such parties. Coffee parties. Mrs O'Henry invites you to a party, then you will have to invite her to a party —'

'Yes, then what?' Uma is defiant. She rubs her nose with the flat of her hand and makes it gleam with defiance. 'Isn't that what you do with your friends — go to their homes for dinner, then invite them to ours?'

Papa's frown has grown so deep he has become locked inside it, he can't emerge into speech, and Mama speaks for him because displeasure always makes *her* articulate.

'That is different,' she says, waving a hand as if dismissing a fly. 'That is because of Papa's work. We have to invite certain people, and we have to visit them. But where is the need for you to go running after Mrs O'Henry?'

'Papa has retired — he doesn't have any work,' Uma flares up, 'and still you go to dinner parties and to the club. And I don't go running after Mrs O'Henry — she invited *me* — you heard her.'

'Why does she keep telephoning you?' Papa speaks up, needled beyond endurance at this mention of his retirement. He has kept his office open, has his clerk come twice a week to do his correspondence, and does not like to think his life is in any way diminished by such a thing as retirement. What would become of his status, his standing, in this town or even in his family, if he gave up these vestiges of his authority and power? It could not be permitted. It must be nipped immediately in the bud. He lowers his brow and directs his blackest look at Uma. 'Is she trying to get you to —'

'Papa,' Uma interrupts in exasperation, 'what can she get from *me?* She only wants me to come and meet other ladies she has invited for coffee!'

'Tchch,' Papa says disgustedly, turning his head away as if it is no use talking to someone as naive and as backward as his older, his *old* daughter.

'It is not good to go running around. Stay home and do your work — that is best,' Mama opines with an air of piety.

'I do my work all the time, every day,' Uma cries tearfully. 'Why can't I go out sometimes? I never go anywhere. I *want* to go to Mrs O'Henry's party.'

Mama summons up all her patience and tries another tack. 'When we tell you to come to the club with us, you won't come. You don't want to come. So now why are you running to Mrs O'Henry? These Christian missionaries — they really know how to entice simple people, and you don't understand they want something from you *in return.*'

Uma is amazed. 'From me? What can Mrs O'Henry want from *me? She* gives me her Christmas cards, *she* sends us Christmas cake —'

MamaPapa exchange looks. Then Papa says, 'Can't you *think?* She is trying to convert you of course.'

Uma gasps. She tries to digest this idea. It is so grave, it takes time to comprehend. When she does, she becomes agitated, as if she is trapped. 'Convert me? What makes you say that?'

Mama sits forward and her face narrows. 'What does she give you all those cards for — those angels and crosses and things — eh?'

'Mama! Those are just Christmas cards — she knows I collect them. You know I have a card collection. And the angels and crosses — they are Christmas decorations.'

Mama purses her lips as if to say she knows better, and Papa looks darker. But Uma has got to her feet and flounced off to her room and banged the door shut in rage and determination.

Mrs O'Henry has spread her plastic lace tablecloth over the low table in her dim, somewhat bleak drawing room with its few pieces of battered wicker furniture and gloomily green curtains. On it she has placed plates with sandwiches and cakes and a coffee pot with only a small chip knocked off its spout. The sandwiches are made with peanut butter and the cakes are called cookies and are very dry. The guests giggle as they try to bite into these rocky lumps, and Uma flushes, feels she must make up for their impoliteness.

'Very nice,' she nods at Mrs O'Henry, holding one in her hand and, with her feet planted apart on the cotton rug, tackles it with every show of pleasure. 'Where did you get from — Bhola Ram's?'

'Oh no, not that Bhola Ram,' Mrs O'Henry dismisses the name of the local baker with the greatest scorn. 'I order my peanut butter from Landour and the cookies are baked according to a recipe in the Landour cook book. The ladies in our mission wrote it especially for Indian conditions, you know, which are different from those at home. But they have lived in this country for a long time and they know what ingredients are available and how Indian ovens work. They've taught a local grocer to make peanut butter, and pickle relish, and blackberry jam, and other things for folks like us. It sure helps.'

'Pickle relish?' one lady enquires, through sticky lips and teeth coated with peanut butter.

'Yes, pickles like you have, but sweet, not hot.'

'Sweet pickles?' the lady explodes with astonishment.

Uma flashes her an angry look through her spectacles. Her spectacles are very expressive. 'It must be nice,' she says, and swings one leg over the other inside the tent of her flowered sari. 'One day I will try to make it. Papa is fond of sweets.'

Mrs O'Henry throws her a grateful look — Uma is certainly the most promising of that circle of ladies. Perhaps because she has had some years at the convent school? Not that nuns are the best influence for young people. 'You should persuade him to send you to Landour one summer,' she says. 'It's real nice, up in the mountains. Cool. Real refreshing.' She sighs and looks up at the slowly revolving fan which has a squeak and a rattle they have never managed to get rid of. 'One needs to get away, from time to time,' she sighs again, with real feeling. Mrs O'Henry has two shining braids of hair that cross over the top of her head and are pinned neatly in place, but her eyes have wrinkles around them and are so faded that they are the colour of washed pebbles.

'Once we went to Simla,' one of the ladies ventures. 'But the water there is not good. My children fell ill.'

'Uh-oh,' Mrs O'Henry says with automatic sympathy.

'Yes, they had very bad diarrhoea. Very bad. With great difficulty we brought them back by train. My husband said better not go again if they only become ill.'

'I always feel *better* when I am in the mountains,' Mrs O'Henry insists and the washed pebbles of her eyes come to life momentarily. She turns to Uma who seems the most likely to sympathise. 'All of us from the mission collect there from all over India, in the summer. It's great. We have concerts and lectures; we get visiting preachers from other parts, to talk and show us slides. At the end of June there's a big fair at

Woodstock School. Folks come all the way from Mussoorie for the fair. Last year, I was in charge of the Christmas card stall. Guess how much I made? For the church? Two hundred rupees in one morning!'

'For the church?' the incorrigible ladies twitter.

'You made the cards yourself?' Uma says. 'Please show us — I would like to learn.'

And Mrs O'Henry seems greatly relieved to lead them away from the coffee table to the latticed veranda at the back where she works. She sets out her coloured papers and scissors and sequins and ribbons and stencils and, instead of educating the ladies in the appreciation of peanut butter and cookies, she is able to impress them — or at least Uma — by a demonstration of leaf-pressing and stencilling.

When they leave, the ladies laugh gaily all the way back to their own homes and families where no one expects any such talents or expertise from them, but Uma clutches a large envelope full of Mrs O'Henry's failures, each pressed fern and violet and pastel paper frill to be added to her collection — tokens of a fairytale existence elsewhere. Elsewhere. Elsewhere.

On saying goodbye, Mrs O'Henry asks her, 'Now isn't your brother in the States?

At a university there? Mr O'Henry said something to me —'

'Oh yes,' Uma nods, 'Arun is at the University of Mass-a-chew-setts,' she enunciates carefully.

'My!' exclaims Mrs O'Henry. 'I've got a sister lives in Massachusetts. It's real cold there in the winter, she says. Hope he's warm!'

Uma nods and goes off down the drive. What fills her head is the idea of Landour — would she ever dare to ask Papa to let her go there, perhaps together with kind Mrs O'Henry?

On seeing her parents' faces when she returns, she puts the idea away along with the cards, at the top of her cupboard.

∞

If one word could sum up Arun's childhood — or at least Uma's abiding impression of it — that word was 'education'. Although this was not what loomed large in the lives of his sisters — who were, after all, being raised for marriage, by Mama, competently enough, or at least as well as she could manage considering the material at hand — if there was one thing Papa insisted on in the realm of home and family, then it was education for his son: the best, the most, the highest. Was this not what his father had endeavoured to provide for him and his brother Bakul, and had it not been the making of them? So what Uma remembered most vividly was seeing him set off for St John's School, his thin legs emerging sadly from his wide khaki shorts the way his scrawny neck did from his khaki shirt; he was often still coughing or snuffling or purplish from the last round of illness, his hand compulsively tearing at a tie round his neck reduced to little more than a string but still an essential part of his equipment. He carried his bag of books and pencil boxes and geometry tools as a coolie might stagger along under an oversized load. Then he staggered back, late in the afternoon, ink on his fingers, chalk on his clothes, socks slipping down into his grey canvas shoes, to the glass of milk that was Mama's contribution to his education — and after that it was the turn of the tutors.

Tutors came in a regular sequence, an hour allotted to each, for tuition in maths, in physics, in chemistry, in Hindi, in English composition — in practically every subject he had already dealt with during the hours at school. Uma and Aruna were warned to keep away, not to provide the faintest dis-

173

traction, but Uma often peeped into Papa's office room which was given over, in the afternoons, to Arun's education. There he sat, at Papa's desk, squirming, chewing his pencils down to the lead, his erasers to mousy shreds of rubber, while the tutors leant back in Papa's armchair, some fiddling inside their ears with a pencil, others scratching dandruff out of their hair in clouds, or wiggling a foot frantically up and down under the desk, to help them through the rigours of drumming theorems, dates, formulae and Sanskrit verses into Arun's head which began to look like one of the rubbers he liked to chew, or the bitten end of a pencil.

The sun would have sunk, there would be perhaps half an hour left of dusty daylight — in the summer, but not in the winter — when Papa would stride into the office, see off the last of the tutors (who also got the very last dregs of Arun's dwindling attention), and magnanimously tell Arun, 'Now go and play. Go and stretch your legs. Have a game of cricket — or something.' Arun would rise creakily to his feet, scrabble together his books and notes in a great pile, and shuffle off to his room with the gait of a broken old man. Throwing them down in a series of dull thuds, he would himself collapse onto his bed, limply put out a hand to lift a comic book from a stack of Supermans and Captain Marvels, and disappear under it. Papa would shout, 'Son! Bring your badminton racquet out — or your cricket bat. You must have some exercise — healthy mind, healthy body —' but Arun would not stir, and Mama would make a little clucking sound of sympathy and prevent Papa from dragging him out bodily.

Then there were the exams when the pace of study would work itself up in its annual crescendo, the tutors in a frenzy, having to make sure their wards performed creditably in order to ensure another year of lucrative tuitions, Arun staying up night after night, sunk into his books while mosquitoes hovered above his head and perspiration slid stickily down his collar. Papa sat out on the veranda, perspiring too, bags collecting under his eyes with weariness but by his vigilance making certain that Arun would not slacken.

After the last of the school examinations — the most frenzied, the most panic-stricken, the most gravely consequential of all — Mama and Uma thought that at last the boy would be free. Mama had ideas about sending him to Aruna in Bombay for a little holiday. Papa treated the suggestion with contempt. 'Holiday? in Bombay? Is that what will get him into a good university? He has to take his entrance tests now, he has to prepare his applications, we have to make lists, collect information —' and it was Papa's busiest time, bustling around to the club, meeting old friends he had not seen in years, gathering advice, references, information, sending Arun off to the bank, the post office, signing statements, filling in applications: there was no end to the paperwork involved, if Arun were to go abroad for 'higher studies'.

'Where is the need?' Mama protested. 'He can go to Seth Baba Ram College here — Mr Joshi went there — it is not bad —'

Papa did not even bother to counter Mama's arguments; he did not expect her to understand the importance of sending Arun abroad to study, the value of a foreign degree, the openings this would create later in life, the opportunities. He merely brushed aside her protests and concentrated on Arun who required all the advice and careful handling Papa could summon. Perhaps Papa's memories of studying under the streetlights and of the painful beginnings in dusty provincial courts filled him with this almost manic determination. Was he fulfilling through Arun a dream he had had there under the streetlights, or in the shabby district courts? Uma watched, trying to find out. Of course he would never tell: how could Papa admit he had unfulfilled dreams? That he had done anything less than succeed, totally?

So when the letter of acceptance finally arrived, Papa it was who collapsed from sheer exhaustion. He was not even able to rise to a celebration, the festivities he had promised his son if he won this prize. He lay back weakly on the swing, his face grey, and allowed Mama to take over and have her way.

But after the first congratulatory embrace and the making of traditional sweets to be sent around to friends and neighbours, Mama too huddled up on the swing, sniffling delicately into her handkerchief, now and then dabbing at her eyes. Uma sat by her, even patted her on the arm now and then, but was uncertain if Mama was sorrowing at the thought of Arun going away, or if this were a role mothers had to play — in which case she must be allowed to continue.

Uma watched Arun too, when he read the fateful letter. She watched and searched for an expression, of relief, of joy, doubt, fear, anything at all. But there was none. All the years of scholarly toil had worn down any distinguishing features Arun's face might once have had. They had left the essentials: a nose, eyes, mouth, ears. But he held his lips tightly together, his nose was as flattened as could possibly be, and his eyes were shielded by the thick glasses his relentless studies had necessitated. There was nothing else — not the hint of a smile, frown, laugh or anything: these had all been ground down till they had disappeared. This blank face now stared at the letter and faced another phase of his existence arranged for him by Papa.

Uma gave a sigh of disappointment and turned away, ungratified. She should have expected no more. It was the expression with which he had gone through several hundred comic books in his childhood — tales of adventure, wizardry, crime, passion, daring and hilarity — allowing them to flood into his mind and drown there in a deep well of greyness that was his actual existence. Uma could gaze into the well, looking for some scraps of coloured paper that might still float, but they had sunk without a trace. Sometimes she was seized with a longing to stir up that viscous greyness, to bring to life some evidence of colour, if not in her life then in another's.

It made her spectacles flash, it gave her movements an agitated edge, but no one noticed. She went back and forth, getting Arun's clothes ready, packing and repacking them. Mama could not summon up the energy required by the task.

Arun paid her little attention, he was too engrossed in the brochures and booklets sent him by the university, trying to picture himself on that strange campus.

Then the day of departure arrived, and he was getting into the train to Bombay from where he would leave for the States. Looking back, he saw Uma on the platform beside his parents and suddenly noticed how old she looked: his sister Uma, already beginning to stoop and shrink. He threw her a stricken look.

With Arun gone, Papa retired. Life was more confined than ever to the veranda, the swing, the intermittent exchanges, the gaps between them longer and longer.

Arun's letters arrived, pale blue aerogrammes. They would finger the crisp glossy paper in turn, marvelling at its quality that somehow endured through the journey. It seemed like evidence of Arun's own endurance, his survival. His actual message, written on the inside, was not nearly so potent. The few lines he wrote sounded thin, without substance. 'I am keeping well. How are all of you? Hope you are well. What is the weather like? Here it is hot —' or cold, or wet, or snowing or hot once again. 'I am studying hard. I have two papers to write this week. We are going on a field trip next week. I am enjoying my studies.' The most personal note he struck was a poignant, frequently repeated complaint: 'The food is not very good.'

He might just as well have written that from the local college hostel, Uma thought in disappointment.

Eleven

Uma has spread all the writing materials out on the table, first removing the embroidered tablecloth so as not to stain it with ink, or have it cramp her writing. She draws up a chair and bends over it, lips clenched inwards as she waits for Papa to begin dictating the letter. She knows she must get it right: the aerogramme costs money, it cannot be torn up like a sheet of paper and thrown away, a fresh one used instead. Papa has warned her about this over and over again. There is a silence, filled in by the constant muttering of pigeons seated on the rolled-up mats; their voices sound like warnings to Uma. She squints at them in irritation.

'Now where are you looking? Just concentrate on the letter, Uma,' Papa scolds.

'I am, Papa, I am. What am I to write?'

'Write "Dear Arun",' Papa clears his throat, speaking slowly. ' "We are happy to hear you have done well in the examinations and can now take a well-earned rest —" '

'Wait, wait,' cries Uma, frantically trying to get the pen to catch up with the words.

'Oof, you are so slow,' he complains.

'She is slow,' Mama agrees, quite unnecessarily.

But this gives Uma time to catch up; she breathes heavily with the effort.

' "Mr O'Henry has come up with a suggestion. You may remember Mr O'Henry from St John's School —" put that in brackets, Uma.'

Uma had started out writing 'Put that in brackets' and now has to scratch it out. She tries to do this unobtrusively but Papa notices, and explodes. 'Don't you know what brackets are? What did they teach you at the convent?'

'At the convent,' she tells him, looking up, 'the nuns would dictate: "Open brackets, close brackets." So we *knew* —'

'Then how is it you don't know?' he fumes, and goes on quickly. ' "Mrs O'Henry's sister lives in the same town as you. Her name is Mrs Patton, and she has one son and one daughter. Mrs O'Henry has written to her and she is willing to let you have a room for the months you cannot stay in the dormitory —" '

'What kind of rule is this?' Mama interrupts, still fuming over it. 'If students cannot stay in the dormitory, where are they to stay, eh?'

'Oof,' Papa turns his irritation upon her. 'Don't you understand? When the university is closed for the summer —'

'I understand, I understand,' Mama says crossly, 'but where are they to *go? That* they do not say!'

'But Mrs O'Henry's sister has offered —'

'Papa, what am I to write? Am I to write "willing to let you have a room" or "has offered" or what?'

Mama retires in a huff, and Papa turns his attention to Uma, bending forwards to make sure she has not muddled the two versions. His deep frown indicates how great a labour this is, as great for him as for Uma. Both are perspiring, and have to stop to mop their necks and faces frequently. The aerogramme is looking damp and wilted as well; it is not of the same quality as those Arun uses, in America. The pigeons on their roosts continue their scolding, complaining and grumbling.

Mama is the one who droops, holding her

head in her hand; she has a headache. When she hears Papa conclude the letter with ' "Mama and Uma send their love. Yours affly —" ' she sighs and leans back, saying sadly, 'Who knows what this sister of Mrs O'Henry is like? Who knows if she will look after Arun properly?'

Papa glares at her and tells her how fortunate Arun is to have a home offered to him free of charge. Uma cannot resist adding 'O'Henrys are very kind people,' to remind them of all the times they had failed to see what is now so evident. But when MamaPapa both turn to glare at her, she thinks it better to change the subject, in fact, to bring the whole matter to a close. 'Now I am going in,' she tells them, standing up. 'My eyes are paining.'

'Your eyes are paining — after just writing one letter? Oof,' Papa lets her know what he thinks of such weakness.

Uma is indignant. All the indignation of the morning has mounted and now reaches its climax. 'I have told you many times my eyes hurt,' she cries.

Mama agrees with her. 'Yes, her eyes are giving her trouble. She has told me they hurt her. Perhaps she should see a specialist.'

Uma has taken off her spectacles and

stands rubbing her eyes.

'Everyone's eyesight grows weaker as they grow older,' Papa declares. 'Don't you know that? You think *my* eyes have not grown weaker?'

'Yes, but you went to see the doctor and he gave you new glasses,' Mama reminds him.

He settles back in silence, and his face closes to all these annoying hints and suggestions being thrown out by the two women; it is like a gate closing on unwanted visitors.

Papa called Uma to the telephone which stood on his desk in the study. He looked extremely irritated at being interrupted 'in his work'. The less there was of it, Uma observed, the more fiercely he made sure it was known to everyone. 'Those convent nuns,' he grumbled as he handed over the phone with extreme reluctance, 'you must tell them not to keep calling.'

'Keep calling?' Uma cried, and snatched the phone from him — the nuns had never called her before. 'Yes? Yes?' she shouted.

It was Mother Agnes, her voice sounding very faded, as if it were a long-distance call.

'Uma dear,' she crackled, like a paper parcel being opened, 'you know we are getting ready for the Christmas bazaar. Mrs O'Henry from the Baptist mission wants to put up a stall but she needs someone to help her. Would you be willing to, dear? You know we will all be busy ourselves with the games and food stalls and the concert —'

Uma was so willing that she was able to ignore Papa's glare totally as she shouted into the phone, 'I'll come, Mother, I'll come.' When she turned around to go and tell Mama, she found Mama in the doorway, listening, so that they nearly slammed into each other.

But in spite of her, in spite of them, it was a day to remember. It was a day as all days ought to be, not just a single one in the whole year, a single one in a whole lifetime. If Uma was asked to paint a picture of heaven, then heaven would have paper lanterns hanging from the trees along the drive and around the school courtyard, pots of white and yellow chrysanthemums like great boiled eggs in freshly painted flowerpots on the veranda stairs. It would have Tiny Lopez's band playing 'Rudolph the Red-nosed Reindeer' and 'Away in a Manger' in a marquee on the netball field. It would have stalls all along one length of it, where ladies stood frying potato fritters, and selling toffees in packets of crinkly pink crêpe paper, bottled drinks and candy floss. It would have stalls all along the opposite length where girls in blue slips and white blouses and ribbons supervised games of chance — lucky dips, pin-the-tail-on-the-donkey, toss-the-hoop, guess-the-weight-of-the-plum-cake. It would have nuns twittering with unaccustomed glee, schoolgirls shrieking to each other down bustling corridors, and someone cranking up a gramophone to play old 45 r.p.m. records like 'My Darling Clementine' and 'The Donkey Serenade'. And Uma would have her own place in that heaven, beside the Baptist missionary's wife with her two braids of shining golden hair, not only permitted but asked to handle the little packets of cards stencilled with leafy ferns or decorated with satin bows, sequin stars and pressed violets. She would collect money in a tin for the flushed and pleased lady who would smile and smile whenever anyone put some more money into it, and who would say, at the end of the day, to Mother Agnes, 'What a fortune we've made for the poor! Every card sold. This *dear* girl has been such a help.' For a treat, for a prize, she would be given a free chance at the lucky dip — and come up with a cloth-bound volume of Ella Wheeler Wilcox's poems, only slightly soiled, to take home as a memento.

Mama did not come to the bazaar. Mama rarely went anywhere without Papa, and then it was only to social events — a bridge evening at the club, or a wedding reception for a friend's daughter. Now that Papa was at home all day, the surreptitious visits to the neighbours' for a round of rummy were no longer possible. If anything needed to be communicated to Mrs Joshi, it was ayah or mali or, now and then, Uma who was sent across with a message. Mama did not object to Uma visiting the neighbours, as long as it did not happen too often, or without her knowledge.

After all, they had known Mrs Joshi ever since she came to the house on the other side of the hedge as a bride, and when her mother-in-law was still alive and still ruled that house like an evil empress of ancient history, able to shrivel the entire garden with her touch, turn sherbet into tepid water, children's games to punishment. The young Mrs Joshi had often slipped through the hedge and come to Mama to complain, even cry a little. But her tears had never lasted, her complaints were overtaken by laughter: she had an endless fund of good humour that made her cheeks fill out and turn round like buns even while she was complaining that she could not drink milk or eat sweets without the evil one criticising her for being greedy. The problem was that this woman's son loved his wife. One could see it in the half-smile that hovered about his face whenever she was near, the way he contrived to smuggle her out of the house and take her to the cinema, the way the two would murmur together and giggle helplessly while the old lady glared futilely. It was what kept Mrs Joshi's eyes so bright, her cheeks so plump. And she was always willing to be drawn into the girls' bedroom and look at Aruna's latest purchases and admire Uma's collection of glass bangles. 'Wear them, Uma, wear them. Why do you hide them away in your cupboard?' she would ask. She never came without some little gift she had managed to smuggle out of the house, and always enquired tenderly after cousin Anamika, having heard how she too suffered at the hands of a mother-in-law as wrathful as her own. When that one finally died, young Mrs Joshi went through all the ceremonies and rituals with impeccable propriety, then took over the household with great aplomb, attaching the bundle of house keys to her own waist, and so began her own benevolent rule.

Where, under the old tyrant, there had been nothing but dust and desolation around the big house, Mrs Joshi now had a bed of roses bloom in her front garden while at the back were beds of fresh vegetables, so profuse and luxuriant that their bounty was shared with all the neighbours.

Her children played all over the place freely: the boys' cricket bats and balls littered the verandas, and swings hung from the big trees. The boys won prizes at school, got jobs, moved to the big cities. The daughters were married off, one after the other, and were now bringing up their own children, teaching in nursery schools, painting or block-printing on textiles, giving or taking music lessons, and leading lives that seemed as easy and light as the flight of sparrows. Only the youngest, Moyna, had inexplicably developed a desire to 'be different', to have 'a career'. They had all been surprised, a little amused, and indulged her little whim. She was off in Delhi, pursuing 'her career', and they laughed, waiting for her to return.

After she had left, Uma would put her arms around Mrs Joshi, nuzzling her freshly powdered neck, and tease, 'Won't you adopt me, Aunty? Won't you let me be your daughter now Moyna is gone?' and Mrs Joshi would reply, laughing, 'Of course! Stay here, be my daughter,' then give her a gentle nudge in the direction of her own home, with a basket of mangoes or a jar of pickles for Mama.

A career. Leaving home. Living alone. These troubling, secret possibilities now entered Uma's mind — as Mama would have pointed out had she known — whenever Uma was idle. They were like seeds dropped on the stony, arid land that Uma inhabited. Sometimes, miraculously, they sprouted forth the idea: run away, escape. But Uma could not visualise escape in the form of a career. What was a career? She had no idea. Her vision of an escape, a refuge, took the form of a huge and ancient banyan tree with streaming grey air roots, leafy branches in which monkeys and parrots feasted on berries. Sometimes she heard the berries raining down on the zinc roof which baked in the clean white sun. Down below there was a river where the sand glistened and a trickle of water gleamed (not the broad, deep, inexorable river running by their own town that had once parted to take her in and draw her away and from which she had been

191

violently torn). She heard the sound of the water jar being set down on the veranda floor. When she closed her eyes, the small motes that drifted through the darkness turned into kites, circling and soaring on air currents, at a great elevation. Then she saw herself seated on a stone step, listening to the parakeets in the banyan tree, looking out at that flash of water in the sand and the kites hovering in the sky so high above that they merged with infinity.

But then she would feel Mira-masi's hands descend on her shoulders and grasp her, and hear her voice intoning, 'You are the Lord's child — I see His mark on you,' or 'The Lord has rejected the man you chose — He has chosen you for Himself,' and Uma would give a start, then begin thrashing her arms around and looking about her wildly, making Mama cry, 'Uma, what's the matter? Uma?' and she would subside, and as she subsided, feel herself drawn by an undercurrent into a secret depth, so dark that she could see nothing at all — just the darkness.

Twelve

All morning MamaPapa have found things
for Uma to do. It is as if Papa's retirement is
to be spent in this manner — sitting on the
red swing in the veranda with Mama,
rocking, and finding ways to keep Uma occupied. As long as they can do that, they themselves feel busy and occupied. She has to
write a letter to Arun, to find out if he has received the parcel containing the tea and the
shawl they sent him through Justice Dutt's
son. In between she has to drive off the urchins who are after the ripe mulberries on the
tree by the gate, and see if the cook has
bought the green mangoes for pickling and
has all the ingredients and necessary spices
— but no extra that might be pilfered. Then,
when Papa says his winter woollens must be
spread out in the sun and sprinkled with dry

neem leaves because he has seen moths hovering about them, Uma, who feels dusty and irritable from her many forays down the drive to the gate to shout at derisive little boys from the street and around to the kitchen to listen to the cook complain about having to get to the bazaar when his bicycle is broken and has not been repaired — Uma thumps her hands down on the table in front of the red swing, the table with the faded embroidered cloth dating back to her school days and sewing lessons with Sister Philomena, and stares into their faces with open defiance. She gives her nose a hard rub with the palm of her hand for extra emphasis. 'Not today,' she tells Papa loudly. 'Can't do it today.'

She walks off to her room and shuts the door behind her. She knows that when she shuts the door MamaPapa immediately become suspicious. But she defies them to come and open it. She stands waiting for them to shout, or knock. Minutes pass and she can picture their faces, their expressions, twitching with annoyance, with curiosity, then settling into stiff disapproval.

She opens her cupboard and considers her belongings. She could look through her collection of cards again but that is a pleasure reserved for holidays, evenings when MamaPapa are out, not just odd half-hour breaks in the routine. She could look through her collection of bangles, or handkerchiefs, but she can do that without shutting the door since Mama would not consider that subversive or dangerous. She could write a letter to a friend — a private message of despair, dissatisfaction, yearning; she has a packet of notepaper, pale violet with a pink rose embossed in the corner — but who is the friend? Mrs Joshi? But since she lives next door, she would be surprised. Aruna? But Aruna would pay no attention, she is too busy. Cousin Ramu? Where *was* he? Had his farm swallowed him up? And Anamika — had marriage *devoured* her?

She stands chewing her lip thoughtfully, then reaches out and picks out the small cloth-bound book she won at the Christmas bazaar. Yes: her lips purse with satisfaction.

She sits down on her bed and lifts her feet up in a comfortable cross-legged position. She can hear the swing creaking and rocking out on the veranda, but the sound fades away when she opens the book and starts to read. She reads slowly, for lack of practice, and she is conscious that she may be interrupted at any minute, called away. But she will read a poem or two, and find the pleasure they deny her. Her lips move as she makes her way through the lines.

'Before this rosebud wilted
How passionately sweet
The wild waltz swelled and lilted
In time for flying feet!'

Her toes twiddle with delight, and she
thumps her knees to the rhythm.

'How loud the bassoons muttered,
The bassoons grew madly shrill;
And oh, the vows lips uttered
That hearts would not fulfil.'

She cradles the book in her lap and riffles
through the thick, soft pages.

'You are wasting your life
    in that dull, dark room
(As he fondled her silken folds);
O'er the casement lean
    but a little, my queen,
And see what the great world holds.
Here the wonderful blue
    of your matchless hue
Cheapen both sky and sea —
You are far too bright
    to be hidden from sight
Come fly with me, darling — fly.'

Outside Mama is shouting, 'Uma! Uma!

Papa wants cook to make him a cup of coffee.'

Uma is frowning over the words: matchless, silken, casement, queen. She will not listen to Mama.

'Coffee — for Papa! Uma!'

Finally Uma throws an angry look at the door. Mama's voice is battering it, sharp as an axe. She hears the door splintering, waits for it to give way. Till it does, she will not move. She tightens her hold on the book. She strokes the cover, opens it to the title page, reads the author's beautiful, melodious name: Ella Wheeler Wilcox. Then the publisher's, equally enchanting: Gay & Hancock, at Henrietta Street, Covent Garden, and the list of other books by the author: *Poems of Pain, Poems of Cheer, The Kingdom of Love, Yesterdays*. . . . If only she could find and read them all.

But now Mama's hands are slapping at the door. 'Why have you locked the door, Uma? Open it — at once!'

Uma gets off the bed and goes quickly to the door, on bare feet, holding her book. She throws it open so violently that Mama stumbles in, almost falling. She steadies herself against the door and, to recover her dignity, demands, 'What is going on here?'

197

Uma thrusts the book into her face: Ella Wheeler Wilcox's *Poems of Pleasure*. Through clenched teeth, she hisses, 'Reading — this!'

Mama bats it away like a fly after a quick, short-sighted glance. 'Reading, reading — didn't you say your eyes were hurting? So now why are you reading? Put it away and fetch a cup of coffee for Papa. It is time for Papa's coffee and biscuits,' she adds very loudly as if afraid Uma will refuse.

Uma does not refuse. She slaps the book down on the table so that her hair brush and bottle of hair oil jump. She walks past Mama and goes towards the kitchen.

She returns to the veranda with a tin tray — the cook has started pickling and won't be interrupted — and puts it down on the table in front of the swing. She sloshes some milk into the coffee. 'Rosebuds. Wild waltz. Passionately,' she screams at them silently. She tosses in sugar. 'Madly. Vows. Fulfil,' her silence roars at them. She clatters a spoon around the cup, spilling some into the saucer, and thrusts it at Papa. 'Here,' her eyes flash through her spectacles, '*this,* this is what I know. And you, you *don't.*'

He takes the cup from her, too startled to protest.

In later years, Mira-masi's visits became more and more infrequent. When she came, she looked gaunt, ill, and her grey hair streamed open down her back, giving her a dishevelled appearance that was a little frightening. Uma was more hesitant in her approaches than she had been, not certain if the bond formed between them by the stay in the ashram still existed. Mira-masi gave no indication if she thought it did; she mostly ignored Uma, although Uma went out into the garden at dawn to collect flowers for her morning rituals, ripping off bright canna lilies and livid hibiscus flowers for lack of anything more suitable for the altar, and Mira-masi did not seem to notice, or care. When Uma asked what she might bring her to cook — the veranda hearth was always swept and cleaned and repaired with fresh clay when Mira-masi arrived — Mira-masi only shook her head: she would cook nothing. 'But what will you eat?' Uma asked anxiously, suppressing selfish thoughts of the sweets Mira-masi had once made for them so willingly and lavishly. 'You must cook something, masi. You don't look

strong. I'll bring you spinach, corn-meal —
what would you like?' Mira-masi only shook
her head. 'I've brought enough food with
me,' she snapped, and produced from the
folds of her cloth sling some bananas and
peanuts and a few shrivelled dates: it was all
she would eat.

She still stalked down the road to the pink
temple at the end, but with such an air of determined privacy — as if defying the others
to stop her or accompany her — that Uma
did not dare follow. Instead, she hovered
around the gate, waiting for her to return,
and pretending to supervise mali in digging
new channels to carry water to a bed where
papaya trees had been planted, or to the jasmine bushes that had to be kept alive
through the summer drought.

The night before Mira-masi left, Uma
crept up to her as she lay stretched out on
the rush mat, and murmured, under cover
of darkness, 'Masi, did you find him — your
Lord?' because the idol was still missing
from the altar.

Then Mira-masi let out a sigh so deep it
seemed to tear the heart out of her chest.
Folding her hands together, she began to
pray for the return of her stolen idol, her
Lord, her lover, her god, in tones of such an-
guish that Uma crawled away in order not to

hear. She was afraid Mira-masi might become hysterical.

As for herself, she no longer had fits: it was as if the plunge into the river had caused the fits and hysterics to be carried off by the currents, leaving her limp and drained. She knew they would not come on her again.

Setting off for the railway station next day, looking somehow stronger and more determined, Mira-masi told her in a private moment of leavetaking, 'I will find Him. You wait and see. I will not stop travelling, from one city to another from temple to temple, ashram to ashram, till I find Him.'

Lila Aunty, on a visit, told them the sequel.

'Yes, yes, Mira has found him,' she laughed, making her bangles jingle. In a shop in Benares that sold brassware. The shopkeeper kept him on a shelf as a presiding deity, and garlanded him and burnt incense before him every morning when he opened his shop for trade.

He did not at all want to part with it. He was alarmed by Mira-masi throwing herself at the shelf and sobbing with joy. He had let her in thinking she was an early customer wanting a brass pot to take down to the river, but she wanted only her Lord, nothing

201

but the Lord Himself. 'Not for sale. Go away, Please, it is not for sale,' he begged her, thinking her mad — mad widows were not uncommon in the streets of Benares — but Mira-masi raised such an unearthly row in the narrow lane of the crowded bazaar, people stopped to stare and flocked around, curious to see what it was all about. Mira-masi was able to create such drama about her Lord, her lost Lord, and the dream she had had, in a temple in the Himalayas on a previous pilgrimage, revealing that if she came to this city, visited this bazaar, walked down this lane, this was where she would find Him, and so she had. She acted out her journey, her dream, the discovery; she laughed and wept, the great red mark a priest had drawn on her forehead that morning becoming smeared and running across her face dissolutely, whereupon everyone nodded and agreed that if it was so, if a dream had come true and a prophecy been fufilled, then the Lord was hers. The poor shopkeeper, a peace-loving man, and superstitious too, parted with the idol.

'After all, he could buy a dozen just like that in the shop next to his!' Lila Aunty laughed.

Mira-masi carried off her prize, the whole population of the lane accompanying her through the bazaar for the ritual bath in the river with great cries of 'Har har Mahadev!'

It was rumoured that she had returned to the temple in the Himalayas where she had had her dream, and now lived in its precincts, devoting herself to worship.

Uma listened avidly. Excitement made the palms of her hands sweaty and damp. Her eyes grew round behind her spectacles and rolled in wonder at the story — Lila Aunty told it well. But, after giving a gratified sigh at the conclusion, she said nothing. She knew MamaPapa would never let her visit Miramasi in the Himalayas; it was pointless to ask. They would not meet again.

Only at night the idea that there was someone who *had* won what she desired would come winging through the dark, rustling her awake, sweeping across her and making her sit up so she could see its shadowy passage and watch it fade into the paleness of daybreak, the sound of its beating wings overtaken by the cacophony of the mynah birds in the sun-drenched trees outside.

Mama screwed up her eyes and got to her feet. Staring into the morning glare, she finally said, in a warning voice, 'There's Dr Dutt coming.'

'Dr Dutt?' cried Uma, instantly bundling away the mending she had been given to do and preparing to enjoy the visit.

'Unf,' Papa grunted irritably, although he was doing nothing at all that she might interrupt. He did not say anything — Dr Dutt's father had been the Chief Justice at one time, it was a distinguished family, and if the daughter was still unmarried at fifty, and a working woman as well, it was an aberration he had to tolerate. In fact, Papa was quite capable of putting on a progressive, Westernised front when called upon to do so — in public, in society, not within his family of course — and now he showed his liberal, educated ways by rising to his feet when Dr Dutt dismounted from her bicycle, unhitched the tuck she had made in her sari to keep it out of the bicycle chain's teeth, and came up the steps with her quick, no-nonsense walk.

Uma was sent to make lemonade for Dr Dutt. She did so enthusiastically, throwing in an extra spoon of sugar and humming even when most of it scattered over the kitchen table, bringing forth an angry reprimand from the cook who would be the one who had to explain where all that sugar went, as he reminded her. Uma laughed at him and went out with the lemonade slopping over the tray because pleasure made her steps uneven. She had last seen Dr Dutt at the Christmas bazaar when she had bought a packet of cards at Uma's stall.

'— and this new batch of nurses is already installed in the new dormitory, twenty-two of them, and the Institute has only just realised that it did not employ a matron or a housekeeper to run it for them,' Dr Dutt was telling MamaPapa who sat side by side on the swing and listened with identical expressions masking their lack of interest. Why was she telling them about the nurses' dormitory, the Medical Institute, the arrangements made or not made there? Such talk was neither about their family nor their circle of friends — how could it interest them?

Dr Dutt nodded at Uma as she saw her come out with the tray of lemonade. 'And so I thought of Uma,' Dr Dutt wound up. Uma nearly dropped the tray and steadied it only after half the lemonade had sloshed out onto it.

Mama sat up in agitation. 'Tchh! Look what you have done. What will Dr Dutt think of you? Go and get another glass.'

'No, no, no,' Dr Dutt cried and took the half-filled and dripping glass. 'I came to see Uma and talk to Uma. And I can't stay long. The beginning of term is a very busy time for us, you see. So we really need Uma to come and help us.'

'Help?' Uma gulped, awkwardly sitting down beside Dr Dutt who put her hand on her arm. Dr Dutt's hold was firm. 'Help?'

'Didn't you hear? Didn't you hear what Dr Dutt was saying?' Papa asked irritably.

'No,' said Uma, and Dr Dutt again rattled through the sequence of events that had left the Medical Institute with a new dormitory and new nurses and no one to take care of them while they were in training.

'So, you see, I thought of you, Uma. A young woman with no employment, who has been running the house for her parents for so long. I feel sure you would be right for the job.'

'Job?' gulped Uma, never having aspired so high in her life, and found the idea as novel as that of being launched into space.

Papa looked incredulous and Mama outraged. Dr Dutt still clasped Uma's arm. 'Don't look so frightened,' she urged. 'I know how well you look after your parents. I know how much you helped Mrs O'Henry with her work. I am confident you can do it.'

But Uma was not confident. 'I have no degree,' she faltered, 'or training.'

'This kind of work does not require

training, Uma,' Dr Dutt assured her, 'or degrees. Just leave that to me. I will deal with it if the authorities ask. You will agree, sir?' she turned to Papa, smiling, as if she knew how much he adored being called sir.

But Papa did not appear to have noticed the honour this time. He was locking his face up into a frown of great degree. The frown was filled with everything he thought of working women, of women who dared presume to step into the world he occupied. Uma knew that, and cringed.

'Papa,' she said pleadingly.

It was Mama who spoke, however. As usual, for Papa. Very clearly and decisively. 'Our daughter does not need to go out to work, Dr Dutt,' she said. 'As long as we are here to provide for her, she will never need to go to work.'

'But she works all the time!' Dr Dutt exclaimed on a rather sharp note. 'At home. Now you must give her a chance to work outside —'

'There is no need,' Papa supported Mama's view. In double strength, it grew formidable. 'Where is the need?'

Dr Dutt persisted. 'Shouldn't we ask Uma for her view? Perhaps she would like to go out and work? After all, it is at my own Institute, in a women's dormitory, with other women. I can vouch for the conditions, they are perfectly decent, sir. You may come and inspect the dormitory, meet the nurses, see for yourself. Would you like to pay us a visit, Uma?'

Uma bobbed her head rapidly up and down. She worked hard at controlling her expression; she knew her face was twitching in every direction. She knew her parents were watching. She tried to say yes, please, yes please, yespleaseyes —

'Go and take the tray away,' Mama said.

Uma's head was bobbing, her lips were fluttering: yes, yespleaseyes.

'Uma,' Mama repeated, and her voice brought Uma to her feet. She took up the tray and went into the kitchen. She stood there, wrapping her hands into her sari, saying into the corner behind the ice-box: pleasepleaseplease —

Then she went back to the veranda — warily, warily. Dr Dutt was sitting very upright in her basket chair. She looked directly at Uma. 'I am sorry,' she said, 'I am very sorry to hear that.'

Hear what? What?

Mama was getting to her feet. She walked Dr Dutt down the veranda steps to her waiting bicycle. 'Isn't it difficult to cycle in a sari?' she asked with a little laugh, and looked pointedly at the frayed and oily hem of Dr Dutt's sari.

Dr Dutt did not answer but tucked it up at her waist and stood steadying the bicycle. She did not look back at Uma but Uma heard her say to Mama, 'If you have that problem, you must come to the hospital for tests. If you need the hysterectomy, it is better to get it done soon. There is no need to live like an invalid.' She mounted the small, hard leather seat and bicycled away, the wheels crushing the gravel and making it spurt up in a reddish spray.

Uma stopped twitching her hands in a fold of her sari and looked towards Mama. Hysterectomy — what was that?

Mama came up the steps and linked arms with Uma, giving her an affectionate little squeeze. 'And so my madcap wanted to run away and leave her Mama? What will my madcap do next?'

The next time MamaPapa went to the club and Uma was alone in the house, she slipped into Papa's office room. The phone which had once stood on a three-legged table in the drawing room and then moved to his desk was now locked in a wooden box, but Uma knew where he kept the key. She scrabbled around in the inky pencil box and found it amongst defunct pens and split nibs, unlocked the box and quickly dialled Dr Dutt's number. It was Dr Dutt's residential number and she felt guilty about disturbing the doctor at home on a Sunday evening. But it was an emergency, of a kind.

Dr Dutt did sound a little unhappy at being disturbed. 'Yes, Uma dear,' she sighed, 'I wish your parents had agreed, but what could I say when your mother told me she was not well and needs you to nurse her?'

'Dr Dutt,' Uma cried, 'Mama is not ill. She's not!'

There was a minute's silence. Was Dr Dutt thinking over the situation or was she brushing one of her pet dogs, or drinking from a cup of tea? What did Dr Dutt do in the luxury of her solitude? Uma stood on one leg and wished passionately that she knew.

Finally Dr Dutt's voice emerged, guarded. 'I don't know about that yet — we'll find out when she comes for her tests.'

'She won't, Dr Dutt, she won't. I know it. Mama's all right! I know she is. You can ask Papa —'

'Your mother may not like that, Uma.'

Uma clenched her teeth so as not to let

out a wail of anger and protest that welled up in her mouth like blood when a tooth is drawn. 'Then tell her to come for the tests,' she begged. 'Phone Mama and tell her to come. You will see, she won't.'

Dr Dutt tried to placate Uma. 'Let's wait till she comes, and then we'll see what is wrong. If it turns out nothing's wrong, perhaps we can talk about the job again.'

'But will the job still be there? If the Institute gets someone else — then? Couldn't you tell Mama to be quick so I can get the job?'

Dr Dutt sighed. 'All right. Call her to the phone and I will speak to her.'

'She is out now,' Uma had to admit.

'Oh.' Dr Dutt seemed to put something down heavily — or perhaps there was someone else in the room who did. 'I will telephone her later,' she promised, and rang off.

She did, next day, but Mama did not tell Uma what was said between them, and Uma could not ask. Uma was in disgrace: she had forgotten to lock up the telephone in its box and Papa had returned from the club to find the evidence of her crime staring at him from his office desk.

'Costs money! Costs money!' he kept shouting long after. 'Never earned anything in her life, made me spend and spend, on her dowry and her wedding. Oh, yes, spend till I'm ruined, till I am a pauper —'

Thirteen

Dinner is over, the table cleared. They go out onto the veranda and sink onto the swing which seems to rock upon an ocean of heavy, sultry air that heaves with the expected monsoon. They swing and rock, creaking, waiting for a breath of air or a drop in the sweltering heat before going in to bed, when there is a sudden slump in the air: the electricity, dim enough at the best of times, has switched off and disappeared into the pit of darkness. A collective groan goes up in the neighbourhood — if not exactly audible, certainly palpable. A collective dismayed outrage.

MamaPapa make it instantly audible.

'Go and fetch candles, Uma,' Mama cries in agitation.

'Wait, wait, Mama. It may come back in a minute,' Uma grumbles.

'No, no, it is a major breakdown. Can't you see, even the street lights have gone off? It will take hours to repair.'

'We must inform the sub-station. Go, Uma. Inform, must inform.'

'You want me to walk down to the sub-station in the dark? Now?' Uma squawks indignantly.

'Don't talk like that. Go and tell mali to go.'

'Unf,' groans Uma, getting to her feet heavily. 'He must be sleeping.'

'Wake him then.'

'Mali! Mali!' Uma bellows from the edge of the terrace. No answer comes from the forest of darkness around so she goes down the steps to the lawn. It is not so dark that she cannot make out the familiar path beside the hedge of night-flowering jasmine, or the dusty bush from which pink oleanders hang in bunches, or the trunk of the ancient tamarind tree. Her feet crunch the sparse gravel of the driveway and she follows it to where mali lives in a shack he has built for himself by the garden tap so that he can guard it and use it to maximum benefit. In fact, he tends never to turn it off completely but to let it trickle just a little: it keeps the earth around his shack enviably moist and cool. Greenery thrives in that damp circle when everything else in the garden has died, withered in the summer heat. A small fire smoulders — just a few embers in a pan that he also likes to keep alive, like the garden tap. All around there is a powerful aroma of the cow-dung pats he uses for fuel, and the raw rank odour of the tobacco he smokes in his chilam.

Mali had been a young man when he first came to work for them. He had astonished the children by such feats as climbing the huge tamarind tree and smoking the bees out of a great hive and bringing it down, filled with wild honey. He had entertained them with stories of the brief time he had been a recruit in the army. He had kept Mama pleased with occasional baskets of tomatoes and beans, and by chasing off urchins who swarmed over the guava trees when the fruit was green, and scaring off the girls when they wanted roses to take to the teachers in school. Now he is too old for such activity, such energy. Now he dozes over his chilam by both day and night.

Uma stands at the edge of his private domain and gives a huge, blood-curdling yell. He comes to life with a gratifying start. 'Ji!' he cries and comes crawling out on all fours from his dark, smoky, odorous cave like some misshapen, bowlegged insect. Seeing it is only Uma, he gives a smile as toothless as an infant's. 'Baby?'

'Wake up, wake up,' she shouts, 'don't sleep so much. Thieves and murderers might be around! Don't you see the electricity is gone?'

'Gone? Gone?' he looks about him enquiringly. It is difficult for him to understand the importance of electricity in other people's lives, but he is willing to give it a try. 'Yes, gone,' he agrees with Uma and shakes his head in sympathy with her indignation.

'Go down to the sub-station and ask how long it'll take to repair,' Uma orders. 'Sahib says,' she adds for effect.

'At once! At once!' he assures her. 'Just give me a minute.' He draws back into his shack to collect a length of cloth that he wraps around his head in a turban, then hobbles off down the drive, the turban bobbing in the shadows like a dusty light bulb. He is an aged glow-worm bumbling through the dark.

'Left right, left right,' Uma calls after him approvingly. 'Like a young recruit, mali, like a young recruit!'

His laugh rings out and carries back from the gate where he stops to give a smart salute, but the laugh is the cackle of an old man, cracked and crusty, and Uma cannot see the salute, she is far too myopic.

She fumbles her way back to the veranda and the swing and sits with MamaPapa, staring into the dark. When they hear steps on the gravel and see the gleam of white clothing, they call, 'Mali? Did you go? What did they say?'

But it is not mali. A voice shouts, 'Telegram!'

Telegram?

'Telegram!'

Uma hurries to fetch a torch. She shines it for the man to see his way to the veranda, then shines it on his register which she has to sign. Papa mutters and Mama clicks her dentures in agitation. This is no ordinary occurrence.

They are opening the envelope, taking out the sheet of pink paper with strips of print glued over it, spreading it out to read by the light of the torch when the electricity suddenly comes to life, blindingly, with a thump, and lights up the message: *Anamika is dead.*

Mali is coming up the drive, shouting, 'Bijlee, bijlee — see, it has come!' beaming with toothless pride.

No one answers. The news has struck like lightning although what it reveals has no reality.

The details that make it real follow later.

They learnt that Anamika had risen from her bed at four o'clock in the morning, only a little earlier than she usually did to take the milk from the milkman who came to deliver it at the kitchen door. If anyone heard her, they thought nothing of her moving about at that hour, it was usual. What she did next was not usual. She turned off the gas cylinder they used for cooking. She filled a can with kerosene oil. She unlocked the kitchen door and went out on the veranda. Then she removed her cotton clothing. She wrapped a nylon sari about her. She knotted it at the neck and knees. Then she poured the kerosene over herself. Then she struck a match. She set herself alight.

At five o'clock her mother-in-law woke to hear a whimpering sound. Earlier she had heard a tin can fall and thought it was a stray dog nosing through the garbage outside the kitchen door. At the whimpering sound, however, she got up and went into the kitchen to investigate. Through the screen door she saw a small fire flickering on the veranda. She went out and found Anamika charred, dying.

That was what she said. To the police. To Anamika's family.

What some of the neighbours said was that she herself, possibly in collusion with her son, had dragged Anamika out on the veranda at that hour when it was still dark — possibly before four o'clock — and that they had tied her up in a nylon sari, poured the kerosene over her and set her on fire.

What the husband said was that he had been away on a business trip and returned only that afternoon on hearing the news.

What the mother-in-law said was that she always had Anamika sleep beside her, in her own room, as if she were a daughter, her own child. Only that night Anamika had insisted on sleeping in her own room. She must have planned it, plotted it all.

What Anamika's family said was that it was fate, God had willed it and it was Anamika's destiny.

What Uma said was nothing.

Anamika's parents come, as eventually they have to come, for the immersion of her ashes in the sacred river. Uma goes to the station with Papa to receive them, Mama waits at home. When they arrive, they sit together — not on the veranda, not on the red swing — but on the floor of the drawing room where Mama has had white sheets spread for mourning. MamaPapa try to make Anamika's parents eat, and rest, and talk, but they sit motionlessly, their heads sunk onto their chests, silent. Bakul Uncle who always strode with his head held high and an air of invincible superiority, now seems almost invisible: he has retreated into a grey shroud of sorrow, while Papa recovers his authority and individuality, and shows that he can command. Lila Aunty, who had always awed them by her urban sophistication, her elegance and — it had to be said — her snobbishness, has collapsed into a heap of rags in a corner, and it is Mama who is in charge, active, concerned, showing both sympathy and care. Uma sits clasping her knees and looks across at the earthen jar they have brought with them and placed against the wall with a garland of marigolds about its neck and more marigolds strewn on the white cloth beneath it. She tries to convince herself that it contains Anamika's ashes, cousin Anamika herself, but she cannot. Anamika was forty-five years old that year, two years older than her. She had been married for twenty-five years, the twenty-five years that Uma had not. Now she is dead, a jar of grey ashes. Uma, clasping her knees, can feel that she is still flesh, not ashes. But she feels like ash — cold, colourless, motionless ash.

Suddenly Uma stirs, puts her hand on Lila Aunty's arm, and asks: 'The letter — the letter from Oxford — where is it? Did you — did you burn it?'

'Uma!' Mama's horrified voice calls out. Papa makes a sound in his throat, a cross between a threat and a warning. Fortunately, the parents do not seem to have heard, or, if they have, have not understood: they do not react.

'Are you quite mad, Uma?' Mama hisses later when she has dragged Uma out. 'You must be mad to ask about that letter now.'

'I wanted to know,' Uma mutters, stubbornly.

Very early next day the car takes them to the river's edge. A boatman, standing knee-deep in water, steadies his boat for them. They haggle over the price for some time, an intolerably long time, it seems to Uma, Papa raising his voice officiously, drowning out the drone of recitations from the people who are lining the bank, some ankle-deep and others waist-deep in water, praying to the sun that is a pale white disc lifting over the horizon into the heavy, dull haze of the sky. Uma huddles inside her sari which she has drawn over her head and shoulders as the other women have, and wishes he would for once stop arguing and pay. For once. Finally Bakul Uncle manages to indicate that he is willing to pay the price. 'Then let's go,' says Papa grumpily, and hurries them in as if it is he who has settled the matter.

Anamika's parents climb into the boat very slowly, as if with pain, because they are holding the jar. There are other relatives who have come with them from Bombay — but not Aruna who is in Singapore on a shopping trip with her husband, not Arun who cannot be expected to break off his studies in America and return, and not Ramu who has become a hermit and communicates with no one in the family any more — and then MamaPapa, followed by Uma. Mama begins to complain about the boat as soon as she steps into it: it does not seem safe to her, and they should look for another.

'Mama, sit down,' Uma hisses at her miserably. Mama gives her a look and is about to reprimand her but does not because now she has discovered there is an inch of water at the bottom of the boat, wetting her feet, that requires her foremost attention.

But it is too late to do anything now; the boatman has pushed away from the bank and is slowly raising then lowering the pole in the mud, grunting heavily each time he does so. The boat has swung around when someone hails it loudly. They turn to see a priest wrapped in an orange robe hurrying across the sand, swinging his bowl. He raises an arm and shouts angrily: how can they perform the final ceremonies without him? What are they thinking of? Have they no care for the proprieties? Without him, would the dead find their way to the bliss of salvation? He stands there on the bank, an irate, unkempt man with red, accusing eyes, threatening them with such dire repercussions that Anamika's mother fearfully speaks up and suggests they go back to collect him. The boatman poles the boat back. MamaPapa fume as only they know how to fume, but they have to shift and make room for him. Mama glares but he seems not to notice, and makes his way through the inch-deep water, climbing over several benches to the prow where he seats himself with affronted dignity and, setting out the tools of his trade, begins to recite the prayers. Anamika's parents try to make the responses he demands of them, but they fail: their throats are dry, the words will not come.

Once Uma has got over the disturbance caused by this interruption of private grief, she finds she forgets it altogether. The rhythm of the boatman's oars — he has put away the pole and is rowing them now they are in deeper water — is steady and strong. The glassy water of the river, swollen by rains up in the mountains from which it comes, seems solid, weighty, a huge mass of grief holding them up on its heaving surface, flowing swiftly and unheedingly beneath. The boat goes with the current now, further and further from the bank, drawn along as if by an invisible rope. The sun is rapidly turning from a small white disc like a shell in the sand to a shimmering blur like a fire in full daylight.

Then her eyes fall on the bowed figures seated in the boat — Anamika's parents, MamaPapa, other relatives — and reminds herself. Anamika, Anamika —

She has cried out aloud, she fears, and claps her hand over her mouth, but it is a lapwing on the bank that is crying, frantically, over and over. 'Did-you-do-it?' it cries. 'Did-you, did-you, did-you-do-it?' The figures in the boat are bending low — they are lowering the jar into the river, into the powerful, swirling current where the two rivers meet and meld. For a moment the jar seems to rest on the surface of the water as if it were a pane of glass; then it breaks through. Briefly it remains visible, bobbing like a swimmer trying to keep its head above water, the garland of marigolds floating about its rim. Then as the boat rocks and steadies itself, it sinks. The marigolds float free, then the current carries them away.

The boatman holds his oars across his knees, watching. The priest's recitation rises in a crescendo, till it arrives at a note of triumph. But abruptly he stops reciting, empties his little jars and vessels over the edge of the boat, refills them, wipes his face with a bit of cloth, and tells the boatman, 'Turn back now, it's done.'

Uma suddenly finds a hand clasping hers tightly. It is Mama's. When Uma turns to look she sees Mama's eyes are closed and there are tears on her cheeks. 'Mama,' she whispers, and squeezes the hand back, thinking, they are together still, they have the comfort of each other. Consolingly, she whispers, 'I told cook to make puri-alu for breakfast and have it ready.' Mama gives a sob and tightens her hold on Uma's hand as though she too finds the puri-alu comforting; it is a bond.

The boat wheels around, slowly, with a great swirling of water against its sides. They return to the bank where worshippers still stand praying and bathing, their silhouettes turned by daylight into a common huddle of greys and browns. The boat nudges into the soft clay of the bank, the boatman climbs out to steady it and help them out, one by one. They descend into the shallow, muddy water and huddle with the others, dipping their vessels into the river and emptying them over their heads and garments while the priest intones his prayers.

Those who have completed the rituals climb out and watch from the sandbank. One of them assumes the yogic posture of the salutation to the sun, as stiff as a crane posing against the sky. Another is singing a hymn to the sun in a voice as reedy and high as a bird's. Someone has taken it upon himself to distribute sweets out of a basket.

Uma dips her jar in the river, and lifts it high over her head. When she tilts it and pours it out, the murky water catches the blaze of the sun and flashes fire.

Part Two

Fourteen

It is summer. Arun makes his way slowly through the abundant green of Edge Hill as if he were moving cautiously through massed waves of water under which unknown objects lurked. Greenness hangs, drips and sways from every branch and twig and frond in the surging luxuriance of July. In such profusion, the houses seem as lost, as stranded, as they might have been when this was primeval forest. White clapboard is most prominent but there are houses painted dark with red oxide, some a military grey with white trim, and a few have yellow doors and shutters, or blue. These touches of colour seem both brave and forlorn, picturebook dreams pitted against the wilderness, without conviction.

Outside many of them the starred and striped American flag flies on a post with all the bravado of a new frontier. In direct contradiction, there are the more domestic signs of habitation that imply settlement by generations — the rubber paddling pools left outdoors by children who have gone in, moulded plastic tricycles and steel bicycles, go-carts and skateboards. There is garden furniture and garden statuary — pink plastic flamingoes poised beside a birdbath, spotted deer or hatted gnomes crouched amongst the rhododendrons like decoys set out by homesteaders, conveying some message to the threatening hinterland.

Arun keeps his chin lowered, as nervous as someone venturing alone across the border, but his eyes glance from side to side into all the windows. None of them are curtained. Most are very large. He can look in directly at the kitchen sinks, the pots of busily flowering busy-lizzies, the lamps and the dangling glass decorations. There are so many objects, so rarely any people. Only occasionally a woman crosses one of these illuminated rooms, withdraws. There seems to be more happening in the darkened rooms where the uncertain light of television sets flickers. Here he might see undefined shapes huddled upon a couch, sprawled on the floor. And there is the multicoloured life of the screen, jigging and jumping with a mechanical animation that has no natural equivalent. The windows are shut, he cannot hear a sound.

Now and then a car turns into the road, very slowly because it is a residential area and there are mountainous speedbreakers, then turns into its assigned driveway. A garage door slides up with an obedient, even obsequious murmur, and the car disappears. Where?

Arun knows nothing. He peers around him for footprints, for signs, for markers. He studies the mailboxes that line the drive, leaning into each other, for some indications or evidence. He notes which ones have names written upon them, which ones only numbers. If the mail has not been collected, he squints to find the name on the newspapers and the mail order catalogues stuffed into them.

Shambling along, he notes which house has a large clutter of children's toys — spades, buckets, bats, balls — and which have carefully constructed gardens: the small beds of bright flowers, stone-edged and stranded in huge stretches of immaculate lawn, the clipped hedges, the bird-feeders watched over by murderously patient cats that seem painted onto the scene in black and white.

Tucking his chin into his collar, he ponders these omens and indicators.

A car drives up suddenly behind him, very close, as if with intention. He climbs hastily onto a grass verge. It passes. Why had it done that? Are pedestrians against the law in this land of the four-wheeled?

He turns into Bayberry Lane and walks past more trimmed lawns, more swept drives, till the road slopes down to the last house in the lane, on the edge of the woods below the hill. Here, too, a red-white-and-blue flag flies upon its pole, its rope slack in the summer stillness, and the mailbox holds its measure of junk mail, too voluminous to merit collection. Here, too, the big picture-windows are lit, and the rooms empty, like stage sets before the play begins: is there or is there not to be a play?

He walks around to the side of the house where a basketball hoop holds its ring over his head in speechless invitation to play. As he slouches past the manicured shrubs, he glances into the kitchen window and sees the aluminium sink, the wall cupboards, the tea towels on their rack.

Mrs Patton is there. She is unpacking several large brown paper grocery bags, placing cartons and containers on the counter, slowly and thoughtfully putting away each item after several minutes of holding it and considering it. Arun stands watching her purse her lips and occasionally touch her mouth with a plump, freckled hand before she bends to put away the cat food or open the refrigerator and stack frozen cans into its icily illuminated spaces.

Now she stops, a can of plum tomatoes in her hand, and does not seem to know what to do next. She is frozen, with a stricken look upon her face, like an actress who has forgotten her lines. Although at the very heart of this domestic scene, she seems lost.

Arun climbs the stairs to the door, pats it with the flat of his hand, pushes it open and apologetically lets himself in.

'Ah-roon!' she exclaims with a little, scared laugh. 'Oh, Ah-roon,' she repeats, trying a different tone, less alarmed. 'I'm glad you're back. Dad got home early. He's on the patio, cooking dinner.'

Arun nods, morosely, since this means it is to be steak again, or hamburger: the odour of raw meat being charred over the fire ought to have warned him. It is the pervasive odour of the entire suburb on any summer evening and it had not struck him that the Pattons were making a contribution to it.

Mrs Patton notes his expression and gives

a little groan. 'What will you eat, Ah-roon?' she worries. 'What will *we* eat, you and I?'

What *will* they eat? He looks back at her dejectedly. Neither is capable of changing the situation. Somehow he has found the one person in the land who is in the same position as he; that makes for comradeship, there is no denying that, but it does not necessarily improve anything.

They both stand staring at the can of plum tomatoes she is holding as if it contains the answer. Becoming aware of his gaze, she brightens. 'There was this special offer at the Foodmart,' she confides, 'three for a dollar.'

Fifteen

An irate voice calls from the patio: 'Isn't anyone interested in the bar-be-cue?'

Mrs Patton clutches a bag of lettuce to her chest and her usually mild eyes suddenly look wild behind the rimless spectacles she wears. Arun, too, pauses. Then she murmurs, 'Quick. Wash your hands, dear. Daddy's got dinner waiting,' and the murmur is as an order might be from another, so urgent is it, and eloquent.

When Arun goes to wash his hands in the small washroom under the stairs where there is a sink wedged in between an ironing board and a filing cabinet, and a toilet beneath a shelf loaded with garden tools and pesticides, he notices an uninhabited slipper at the foot of the stairs, just protruding from behind the banister.

On coming out, with damp hands, he takes another look at it, curious. It does not move but he feels impelled to ask, hoarsely, 'Melanie?'

The owner of the slipper does not reply but ruffles a bag she is holding on her lap. He retraces his steps to find her sitting on the bottom stair, dressed in denim shorts and a faded pink T-shirt, holding a party-sized bag of salted peanuts into which she reaches and from which she draws out a fistful. She sits in the gloom of the unlit staircase, munching the nuts with a mulish obstinacy, regarding him with eyes that are slits of pink-rimmed green. Has she been crying? She looks sullen rather than tearful. It is her habitual expression. Arun reflects that he has not once seen it change.

'We are asked to come to dinner,' he mutters, looking away, down at her bare foot beside the empty, dusty slipper, 'by your father.'

In reply she thrusts her fist down into the bag again, crinkling it loudly, and draws out another handful of peanuts. She does not say a word. Perhaps the crunching of nuts is her reply. Certainly she makes it expressive, and defiant.

Stooping even further — this is only the latest in his many failed attempts to involve

Melanie in speech — he goes out through the kitchen door onto what the family calls the patio. At its edge, just under the branches of a large, spreading spruce, Mr Patton has set up his grill at which he stands, garbed in a long, red-checked apron that ties at his neck and descends to his knees. Embroidered across the pocket at the top is the legend *Texas Bar & Grill*. He holds a spatula up in the air, waiting for his congregation to assemble.

It is a congregation of two, hesitant and slow.

'Where's Rod?' he demands. 'Where's Melanie?'

Mrs Patton and Arun exchange looks, furtively, and Mrs Patton goes bravely forward as if to take the shot, and says placatingly, 'I'm sure they'll be here any minute, dear.'

'Don't they know I came home early to cook their dinner?' Mr Patton sounds petulant, a minister who cannot see why his congregation dwindles. His lower lip is moist, like a baby's, and his hands, too, are surprisingly soft, pampered. 'Got my work done, got into the car, and drove home half an hour early so's to marinate the steaks — and then they can't even get here on time to eat.'

Arun stands looking at his shoes, dusty

from the long walk out of town, and carefully refrains from informing him that Melanie is indoors, gorging on peanuts. He waits for the dreaded moment when he will have to confess what he wishes he did not have to confess — again. Will Mrs Patton make the confession for him? Will Mrs Patton be brave and make it unnecessary for him to speak, publicly reveal himself as unworthy, unfit to take the wafer upon his tongue, the wine into his throat?

'Come on, bring me your plates,' Mr Patton tells his foot-dragging communicants, trying to sound jovial and only managing to sound impatient.

Mrs Patton advances, holding her plate before her. She stands very upright before the grill, trying not to flinch but evidently fully aware of the gravity of the ceremony. 'Thank you, dear,' she says as she receives the slab of charred meat on her plate, making it dip a little with its weight so that grease and blood run across it and spread.

'And now you, Aaroon,' commands Mr Patton, sliding the spatula under another slab that is blackening upon the coals. 'This here should be just right for you, Red,' he jollies the nervous newcomer to his congregation, not yet saved but surely on his way. Arun has made the mistake of telling the

Pattons once that his name means 'red' in Hindi, and Mr Patton has seized upon this as a good joke, particularly in conjunction with his son's name, Rod. Fortunately Arun has not elaborated that it means, specifically, the red sky at sunrise or Mr Patton might now be calling him 'Dawn'.

Instinctively, then, Arun steps backwards and even puts his hands behind his back. Some stubborn adherence to his own tribe asserts itself and prevents him from converting. 'Oh, I'll just have the — the bun and — then salad,' he stammers and his hair falls over his forehead in embarrassment.

Mr Patton raises an eyebrow — slowly, significantly — holding the spatula in the air while the steak sputters in indignation at this denial.

Mrs Patton rushes in hurriedly, but too late. 'Ahroon's a vegetarian, dear —' and then her voice drops to a whisper '— like me.'

Mr Patton either does not hear the whisper, or does but ignores it. He responds only to the first half of the statement. 'Okay, now I remember,' he says at last. 'Yeah, you told me once. Just can't see how anyone would refuse a good piece of meat, that's all. It's not natural. And it costs —'

Mrs Patton begins to play the role of a distracting decoy. She flutters about the patio, helping herself to bread and mustard, pattering rapidly, 'Ahroon explained it all to us, dear — you know, about the Hindoo religion, and the cows —'

Mr Patton gives his head a shake, sadly disappointed in such moral feebleness, and turns the slab of meat over and over. 'Yeah, how they let them out on the streets because they can't kill 'em and don't know what to do with 'em. I could show 'em. A cow is a cow, and good red meat as far as I'm concerned.'

'Yes, dear,' Mrs Patton coos consolingly.

'And here it's all turning to coal,' Mr Patton mourns, patting the scorched slice.

Arun follows Mrs Patton to a table set with platters and bowls of lettuce and rolls. Sadly he resigns himself to the despised foods, wondering once again how he has let himself be drawn into this repetitious farce — the ceremonies of other tribes must seem either farcical or outrageous always — as bad as anything he remembers at home. Thinking of his father's stolid face and frown at the table, grave and disapproving, he feels he must assure Mrs Patton as he would his mother, 'I will eat the bun and salad.'

Mr Patton says nothing. He is prying the

scorched shreds of meat off the grill with his spatula and scraping them onto his plate, grievously aware of the failure of this summer night's sacrament.

Mrs Patton settles onto a canvas chair and pantomimes the eating of a meal while playing with it with her fork. 'Mmm, it's real good,' she murmurs. 'Rod and Melanie just don't know what they're missing.'

Her words make Arun wince. Will she never learn to leave well alone? She does not seem to have his mother's well-developed instincts for survival through evasion. After a bit of pushing about slices of tomatoes and leaves of lettuce — in his time in America he has developed a hearty abhorrence for the raw foods everyone here thinks the natural diet of a vegetarian — he dares to glance at Mr Patton. As he expected, Mr Patton's underlip is thrust out in a petulant scowl as he cuts and saws at a piece of meat that to Arun seems not merely raw but living: it is bleeding in a stream across Mr Patton's plate. The air is murky with the smoke of the dying barbecue and the spreading dusk; the blood is a stain, a wound at its heart.

The blue oblong of electric light that hangs from a branch of the spruce tree over the barbecue is being bombarded by the insects that evening summons up from the surrounding green. They hurl themselves at it like heathens in the frenzy of their false religion, and die with small, piercing detonations. The evening is punctuated by their unredeemed deaths.

Sixteen

The room Arun had had in a dorm during that first semester of his American education was on the fifth floor of a fourteen-storey block at the edge of the campus. He shared it with a mostly silent student from Louisiana who would lie on his back smoking an endless chain of cigarettes, filling the small concrete cell with a thick yellow smoke that brought on Arun's asthma. The boy had a coffee mug that bore the legend *Ya snooze, ya lose,* but he used it only to drop ashes in and ignored the message that stared Arun in the face every time he glanced, inadvertently, in his direction.

The room was at the end of a long corridor scribbled over with graffiti — in chalk, charcoal, spray paint, lipstick, possibly even ordure — and its one window, an oblong of uncurtained glass, looked out onto the parking lot. From his desk Arun could look across its bleak expanse, watch students drive off in their cars, leaving behind pools of oil and grease. On Friday nights even this desolation would explode — quite literally — as students hurled beer cans out of the windows, sometimes entire garbage bags filled with them, and bottles were flung down to shatter spectacularly. The emptiness of Arun's weekends would be punctuated by sudden eruptions of music from enormous pieces of sound equipment set up or transported across the campus. These were like voices shouting out of another world, another civilisation:

> 'Hey, hey, baby,
>   I can't let you go-o —'
> 'Don' you mess wid me,
>   Ah'm a fightin' man —'
> 'Boo-hoo, boo-hoo,
>   I'm so bl-ooh, bl-ooh —'

Their very volume created a fence, a barrier, separating him from them. They were the bricks of a wall that held him out.

It was much the same in the classes he attended. After taking a look around the classroom at his fellow students, and noting the young man who wore his hair in a plait, the older woman who had short grey hair on which she always wore a baseball cap, the young girl who hungrily ate her way through packages and cartons full of food, bottles full of coloured liquids, rolls of candy and gum, then finished off with a very ripe banana or almost rotten orange, his instant reaction was to reject them all as potential allies or friends. After that, he could lower his face into his books, hide himself behind his thick glasses, and excuse himself from any further involvement with them.

Once he had run into the older woman from his geology class in the cafeteria: he had not noticed she was sitting at the table till he had already put down his tray beside her and it was too late to be able politely to change his mind.

She beamed at him. 'I missed today's class,' she told him. 'Just got back from the med centre — had to go for my checkup.'

'Oh, are you ill?' he had to ask then.

'Cancer,' she told him, with professional pride, 'of the cervix. They spotted it on time — I've been regular with my pap smear — and I had chemo. That's when my hair fell out.' She put her hand to her head and pulled off the baseball cap, revealing the bald patch beneath it. Arun stood, appalled, but she laughed reassuringly, 'It's growing back now, except for this bit here. My husband wants me to wear a wig, but I say what the hell, I don't care about all that, looking glamorous and such. What I care about is getting me an education.' She put her hand on her book bag with pride, as if swearing an oath of allegiance. 'He doesn't see why. Folks don't always know what the important things in life are. But you know more about that where you come from,' she suddenly broadened out to include him.

Arun immediately panicked, and the straw in his bottle of Coke bent under the pressure of his fingers. As soon as he could, he fled. She had confirmed what it was that filled every cell of his body — a resistance to being included.

He resisted even the overtures made by his own countrymen who had formed a small ghetto on the thirteenth floor of the dorm where they could concoct the foods that they longed for over an illegal hot plate and sing to the tapes of music that were their most precious possession from home. Arun always managed to have a test to prepare for when they invited him to join them for a meal they had made, and a Bombay film they had found at the local video store.

In spite of that, they had generously offered, towards the end of that semester, 'You can join us if you like — we're taking a house for the summer — it'll work out cheap if we share.'

Arun pretended to have other plans. Not quite finalised, he muttered, he'd let them know.

The truth was that he had no plans, only the hope that his time in the US would continue in this manner, that he could always share a cell of a room with a silent roommate who concealed his facial expressions behind a screen of smoke, that he would attend lectures where the lecturer never even learnt his name, and find food in a cavernous cafeteria where no one tried to sit beside him.

It was the first time in his life away from home, away from MamaPapa, his sisters, the neighbourhood of old bungalows, dusty gardens and straggling hedges where he had grown up, the only town he had ever known; he had at last experienced the total freedom of anonymity, the total absence of relations, of demands, needs, requests, ties, responsibilities, commitments. He was Arun. He had no past, no family and no country.

The summer in the US stretched out open, clear and blank. Arun had every intention of keeping it so.

Seventeen

Unfortunately there were two matters he had not taken into consideration.

One was that the dorm needed to be emptied of all students: the university wanted every room back for its summer courses and conferences from which it made a sizeable income, and he would have to move out for the summer.

Having turned down the offer made by fellow Indian students, he was driven to looking for a place on his own: a single room in some featureless housing block was his desire, somewhere he would not run into anyone he knew. He began to look up ads in the local newspaper for rooms to let.

One turned out to be the back of a garage, boarded up into a kind of dog-house, the only window a long narrow panel set up high under the rafters. Arun was not driven away even by such conditions; what did turn him away was the information that he would have to enter the owner's house to make use of the bathroom and kitchen. He withdrew hastily.

Another turned out to be in a hamlet in the woods where he would be alone in a tiny cabin surrounded by miles of conifer trees with the owner and his wife. They beamed at him welcomingly: he fled as from a spider's nest.

He went to the Student Centre on the campus and sat with other students at a long table, flipping through files marked Rooms or Apartments to Let, and passing them up and down to each other. There was a telephone outside the door from where they could telephone the numbers they found in the files as long as their dimes and quarters lasted.

Arun queued up behind them and found: a farmer who was letting a room in a loft at the top of his barn in return for help with the hay, but Arun could not drive a car, let alone a tractor, and had to pass that up; a single mother in a two-roomed apartment who was offering a living room couch in return for baby-sitting her two-year-old-son, and three women who shared a studio apartment and wanted a fourth to help bring down the rent and were offering a divan beside their own beds and could not understand why Arun would not even come to take a look at it.

His dream of a self-contained room in an apartment or housing block where no one would know him or talk to him was disintegrating.

That was when the aerogramme from home arrived, carefully penned by Uma in her square, even handwriting like that of a child doing a writing exercise, but dictated — of course — by Papa. It gave him some information so unexpected that he had to read it a second time before he could digest it: Mrs O'Henry, the wife of the local Baptist missionary (he was Vice-Principal of the school Arun had attended and had written a recommendation to help him win a scholarship in the States), had a sister who lived in a suburb of that very town, and had written to her regarding the problems Arun was having in finding a place for the summer (they were discussing it all the way back *there?* Had they *still* not stopped discussing him, plotting and planning his life for him?) and she had come up with an offer of a room in their house. He was to telephone her and 'finalise it' (Papa's term): it was a kind offer, generously made, and not to be rejected.

Immediately Arun was overcome by the sensation of his family laying its hands upon him, pushing him down into a chair at his desk, shoving a textbook under his nose, catching that nose and making him swallow cod liver oil, spooning food into him, telling him: Arun, this, Arun, that, Arun, nothing but . . .

He floundered, he sank.

His voice on the telephone was so low that Mrs Patton could hardly hear him. 'Oh dear, it's a very bad line,' she piped, 'I can hardly hear you.'

'Umm — I — I'm working in the library here — it's very far from where you live —'

'Oh no, oh no,' she went on piping, 'there's a bus service, you know. You can catch a bus out to us. It's real pretty out here. You'll love it — and I have two youngsters, just about your age, I think.'

He put his hand over his mouth to quell his nausea.

Mrs Patton gave him a pleasant light-filled room on the first floor of the house on Bayberry Lane. It had a white bed, a white chest of drawers, a white rug on the floor and white curtains at the window that looked through the branches of a maple tree at a slope of grass leading down into the woods. When she left him after showing him the closet and the hangers, he stood watching as a squirrel with a long tail emerged, sat on the sloping lawn, seeming to listen to or watch something happening in the woods that Arun could not see or hear, then dropped to its four feet and scurried towards it. The woods seemed to draw closer, settle about the window, looking in. Seeing the string of the shade dangle before him, Arun pulled at it. The shade tumbled down precipitously. The room was dark. He tugged to raise it a little, a few inches from the sill, but it merely fell lower. Now it hung limply from its rail, its full length unfurled.

Fearing he had broken the string, or some spring, and that it would hang there accusingly always, Arun tiptoed guiltily out of the room onto the landing. The door to the bathroom stood open. He could see a corner of the bathtub, a length of shower curtain, a shelf piled with toothbrushes and squeezed tubes of toothpaste, some pots of cream. The other doors on the landing were shut. One bore a pennant proclaiming *Boston Red Sox* and the other a long scratch and a spattering of nail polish.

Gulping, Arun went down to the kitchen again and asked Mrs Patton if there were wild animals in the woods.

'Wild animals?' She stood astounded, dripping jelly from a long-handled spoon, then burst out laughing. 'Oh yes, yes,' she chuckled, 'lots — two-legged ones. They like to play out there after school, and there's a swimming hole at the bottom of the hill. That's where all the kids swim in the summer,' she explained. 'Those aren't *real* woods, you know. To get to the real woods you've got to go all the way to Quabbin. Around here there's just — just trees,' she smiled, with a little flutter of her hands, spraying pink jelly.

Arun gave an involuntary shiver as he felt them creeping up around him, rustling as they closed in.

'I think,' he blurted, 'I've broken the shade.'

Eighteen

There followed an embarrassing scene, but it did not have to do with the shade: that she brushed aside as too unimportant to take up, but said, apologetically, 'You'll be wanting your own kind of food, I'm sure, and I know I won't be able to provide that, my sister's written and told me how different your food is from ours. She's lived there — oh, twenty years or more, and writes me these amazing letters. My, I'm amazed by what she tells me, I am. India — gee!'

'Oh, uh,' he mumbled, wondering how to deal with the dread he had of sitting down to meals with this family of strangers and providing them with amazing stories as well. 'I could — I could eat my meals in town when I go to work — at the library — and before I get back at — uh, night —'

She was both horrified and relieved — he could see that; her face was the most transparent he had encountered: she had no guile at all. He had only to insist a little and he knew she would give in, and he could continue with the blessed anonymity of eating in a cafeteria or buying a sandwich to eat out under a tree.

He tried to establish some routine that would allow him to pursue this line, but it soon became obvious that it was not really possible. The hours he worked at the library were irregular, they did not always include a lunch hour, or extend till dinner-time, and if he was in the Pattons' house in the suburbs, he could not walk all the way back into town for a meal — the nominal bus service having been cut down to its seasonal minimum, something Mrs Patton could not have known since she never used it — or he would be spending most of the summer trudging along the highways, climbing onto grass verges to avoid speeding cars, and eating their dust, and jeers.

As he trailed back in the afternoon dust one day, coming in at the kitchen door and wiping his shoes on the mat, Mrs Patton placed her hands on the kitchen table and faced him. Her hands were brown and square, the skin slack and wrinkled. A wristwatch and gold wedding band on one, a cheap silver ring on the other, no nail polish. She pressed her fingertips on the wooden table and spoke to Arun.

'No, Ahroon,' she said, 'you can't go on going out and walking into town for every meal. Why, what would my sister think? This just can't go on. It's clear you've got to do your cooking and eating here. I know my cooking wouldn't suit you — my sister warned me about that — but if you tell me how you like things, I'll try to fix them just so. You'll only need to tell me how.'

He looked at her miserably: so much kindness, so much goodness, how was he to defend himself? 'I am sure I will like your cooking, Mrs Patton,' he said, choking.

Her eyes gazed upon him, as unbelieving as a young girl's. 'You really think so? I just do plain old home cooking, you know.'

'Oh, Mrs Patton,' he muttered, 'I — I'm a vegetarian.'

Her eager face froze, then retreated. She seemed frightened.

'I — I don't eat meat,' he explained, red-faced. It was all so much more complicated than he had expected — life, travel, escape, recapture.

But while he stared at his shoes, seeing all the dust that lay heavily on them, she had changed, darted into another mood, and now her voice came ringing out, clear and light. 'But I think that's wonderful — I really do. My sister told me many Indians were vegetarians. I've always wanted to be one myself. I've always hated eating meat — oh, that red, raw stuff, the *smell* of it! I've always, always disliked it — but never could — never knew how — you know, my family wouldn't have liked it. But I've always liked vegetables best. My, yes, all those wonderful fresh vegetables and fruit you get in the market — they're so *pretty,* they're so *good.* I could — I can live on them. Look, Ahroon, you and I — we'll be vegetarians together! I'll cook the vegetables, and we'll eat together —'

'Oh, oh,' he tried to laugh. 'Oh no, Mrs Patton, you don't have to do that —'

'No, no, no, I don't have to — I want to. I really, really do. Now I've got a vegetarian living here right in my house, now is the time for me to become one myself. You know, the two of us together —' She laughed, too, easily, like a conspirator. 'I couldn't do it with just — just Dad and the kids, you know. Dad likes his meat, and Rod — well, Rod needs all the proteins he can get, for all that weight-lifting and jogging that he does. And Melanie — oh, Melanie.

No, no — they don't even *eat* vegetables. But now you're living with us, I can cook vegetables at last —'

She ran on as happily and eagerly as if she had discovered a new toy. He began to grow puzzled by her enthusiasm, wondered how he had set it off, having none himself.

'We'll go down to the stores together,' she was saying, 'and stock up on — cereals, and — and spices and stuff. You can show me how to fix a vegetarian meal. It'll be my vegetarian summer,' she ended with a delighted laugh.

Nineteen

And so they began their careers as shoppers, Mrs Patton driving Arun in her white Honda Civic to the supermarkets along Route Two and opening out to him a vista of experience he had never expected to have. He was perplexed to find these stores and their attendant parking lots, bank outlets, gas stations, Burger Kings, Belly Delis and Dunkin' Donuts stranded on huge stretches of tarmac spread upon fields of meadow grass and summer flowers while in the distance the blue hazy line of woods smouldered and smoked against the blazing summer sky. Why would townspeople need to go into the country to shop? he wondered, but when he ventured to ask Mrs Patton, she could only give a little shake of her head and a small smile, not having understood his question: why should anyone question what was *there?*

She had already parked her car, swung out of it with her handbag, and was hurrying past the ranks of parked cars to the nest of stacked shopping carts in her eagerness to begin, while Arun trailed slowly after her, his eyes lingering over the cars that were not what he had previously known as cars — vehicles, designed to carry passengers from one point to another — but whole establishments, solid and rooted in their bulk, all laboriously acquired: weightage, history, even an inheritance. Their backseats piled with baby seats, dog blankets, boxes of Kleenex, toys and mascots adhering to their windows like barnacles. Each a module designed to contain and propel lives and dreams. Numberplates that read:

'I l♥ve my Car'
'Another Day, Another Dollar'

and stickers that proclaimed:

'Guns, Guts and God
Make America Great.'

Histories inscribed on strips of plastic:

260

'My Daughter and I Both Go To
   College,
My Money and Her Brains.'

Certificates of pride:

'Dartmouth.'
'University of Pennsylvania.'
'Williams.'

And warnings:

'Baby on Board'
'I Brake for Animals'
'One Nuclear Accident
   Could Spoil Your Whole Day'

Arun was dizzied by these biographies, these statements of faith. He could have lingered here, constructing characters, lives to go with these containers, all safely invisible, but Mrs Patton was waiting for him at the automatic doors. He could see her in her flat rubber-soled sandals, her yellow slacks and T-shirt that bore the legend *Born to Shop,* her hands on the cart she had chosen. As with his question regarding the location of the super-market, she could not understand what was preoccupying him. 'Everything okay?' she asked as he caught up at last.

Once inside the chilled air and controlled atmosphere of the market, she showed him how to shop by her own assured and accomplished example, all the tentativeness and timidity she showed at home gone from her. He learnt to follow her up and down the aisles obediently, at her own measured pace, and to read the labels on the cans and cartons with the high seriousness she brought to the exercise, studying the different brands not only for their different prices — as he was inclined to do — but for their relative food value and calorific content. Together they wheeled the cart around and avoided walking past the open freezers where the meat lay steaming in pink packages of rawness, the tank where helpless lobsters, their claws rubber-banded together, rose on ascending bubbles and then sank again, tragically, the trays where the pale flesh of fish curled in opaque twists upon the polystyrene, and made their way instead to the shelves piled with pasta, beans and lentils, all harmlessly dry and odour-free, the racks of nuts and spices where whatever surprises might be were bottled and boxed with kindergarten attractiveness. Mrs Patton's eyes gleamed as they approached the vegetables, all shining and wet and sprinkled perpetually with a soft mist spread upon them, bringing out colours and presenting shapes impossible in the outside world. To Arun they seemed as unreal in their bright perfection as plastic representations, but she insisted on loading their cart with enough broccoli and bean sprouts, radishes and celery to feed the family for a month.

'But will they eat?' he asked worriedly as he helped her pull polythene bags off their rollers and open them, then fill and close them with a twist.

'What does it matter, Ahroon? *We* will,' she laughed gaily, at the same time weighing a cantaloupe in her hands and testing it for ripeness.

'Excuse me,' said a voice, and a woman leant over to pick her own cantaloupe: she wore a T-shirt that declared *Shop Till You Drop.*

This unnerved Arun but Mrs Patton did not seem to see.

Her joy lay in carrying home this hoard she had won from the maze of the supermarket, storing it away in her kitchen cupboards, her refrigerator and freezer. Arun, handing her the packages one by one — butter, yoghurt, milk to go in here, jam and cookies and cereal there — worried that they would never make their way through so much food but this did not seem to be the object of her purchases. Once it was all stored away in the gleaming white caves where ice secretly whispered to itself, she was content. She did not appear to think there was another stage beyond this final, satisfying one.

It was left to him to extract what he wanted from this hoard, to slice tomatoes and lay lettuce on bread, or spill cereal into a bowl; she watched, with pride and complicity. Arun ate with an expression of woe and a sense of mistreatment. How was he to tell Mrs Patton that these were not the foods that figured in his culture? That his digestive system did not know how to turn them into nourishment? For the first time in his existence, he found he craved what he had taken for granted before and even at times thought an unbearable nuisance — those meals cooked and placed before him whether he wanted them or not (and how often he had not), that duty to consume what others thought he must consume.

If she noticed his expression, she seemed incapable of doing anything about it. She had provided: she had foraged, she had gathered, she had put forth. Now she stood beaming, her arms crossed over that T-shirt that bore those ominous words, her eyes flashing the message of the bond between man and woman, between woman and child, brought to ideal consummation.

No, he had not escaped. He had travelled and he had stumbled into what was like a plastic representation of what he had known at home; not the real thing — which was plain, unbeautiful, misshapen, fraught and compromised — but the unreal thing — clean, bright, gleaming, without taste, savour or nourishment.

If Mr Patton ever noticed or watched this arrangement between his wife and the Indian boy they were giving shelter to that summer, he never referred to it or acknowledged it. He stopped on his way back from work to shop for steak, hamburger, ribs and chops. 'Thought you might not have enough,' he told Mrs Patton as he marched out onto the patio to broil and grill, fry and roast, and Mrs Patton looked suitably apologetic and deceitful. When she finally brought herself to tell him that Arun was a vegetarian and she herself had decided to give it a try, something she had meant to do for a long time now, he reacted by not reacting, as if he had simply not heard, or understood. That, too, was something Arun knew and had experience of, even if a mirror

265

reflection of it — his father's very expression, walking off, denying any opposition,
any challenge to his authority, his stony wait
for it to grow disheartened, despair — and
disappear. Once again, its grey, vaporous
chill crept into his life, like asthma.

Twenty

The television set flickers with nocturnal life in the darkness of the den. On his way back to his room after the usual fiasco of the dinner, Arun pauses a moment to see what or who is heaped upon the sagging sofa in front of it. It interests him how that heap might draw itself together, separate and present itself. But the steady crunching of peanuts gives away the identity of the viewer without any movement: it is Melanie, Melanie alone, cross-legged upon the plaid cushions with her bag of pea-nuts — surely by now another bag? — stur-dily eating her way through it during a commercial break. He stands at the door and watches advertisements for an insurance company (a young and radiant family floating through a flowery meadow), a dental appliance (a blue-haired lady placing a bowl of cereal before a grey-haired man and embracing him bravely), an automobile (an angelic apparition leaping through a sunset into the dark while below a long, low vehicle proceeds through desert sands and cacti while a choir sings 'The great American road . . . the great American car . . .').

The commercial break shows no signs of breaking. Arun detaches himself from the door to sidle away when Melanie becomes aware of him watching. She turns her pale face towards him and even in the darkness he can read its expression: Get out, it says, and he does.

In his room he has his own television set. Mrs Patton has insisted he have one — perhaps she knows with what ferocity Melanie monopolises the one in the den. His is old, black and white, and occupies too much space on his small desk under the window. In order to work, he has to move it to one corner and somehow ignore its presence. He does so, and stares out of the window: the shade has been raised by someone, he does not know who, and he does not pull it down again. So he must confront the woods, in the dark.

Much later, in the stillness that is underlined by the steady drizzling of the cicadas in the trees, he glances out and sees, on the patio, which seems illuminated because it is made of squares of pale stone, the smouldering remains of the barbecue at its edge. And there is a forager standing beside it, peeling the shreds of leftover meat from the implements that lie scattered about. From the size, the bulk and the clothing, he sees it is Rod. Rod has returned. His hair is still held back by the luminous band he wears while jogging. He is wearing shorts but no shirt, and his chest is wet and gleams, greasily. He is standing there at the edge of the patio, legs apart, gnawing at whatever nourishment he can find.

Arun moves behind the curtain so that he cannot be seen watching.

Still later that night, when he has without knowing it fallen into a deep pit of unconsciousness, he is woken by a brittle clatter. Instantly, he leaps towards the window, clutching his blanket to him. He stares down at the patio, wonders if Rod is still prowling there, in search of victuals.

Instead of Rod, he sees a burglar with the traditional mask over its eyes, small gloved hands helping themselves to the contents of the garbage can. It stands on two feet and only the white bar of fur across its face gives it away in the intense dark. It is prying a hole into a paper bag which crackles. Then it drops to its four feet and disappears into the trees, heavily, as if dragging with it whatever it can take.

Bugs are still hurling themselves at the blue electrocutor with all the frenzy of kamikaze pilots, and meet their deaths with sudden poignant pings and the rush of eerie sizzling in the night.

Having been awakened, Arun decides to slip across the landing before going back to sleep. Opening his door, he is dismayed to see the light is on, shining onto him. Someone has left it on in the bathroom. He hobbles over to the open door, blinking, and receives a second shock. Melanie kneels there at the toilet bowl, in white pyjamas that are printed all over with lipstick marks in the shape of lips, and she is retching heartily into it. She has heard him, or seen his shadow, and swings around frightenedly. Her face is beaded with perspiration, and white as the flesh of a fish fillet in the supermarket. The dark rings under her eyes make her resemble the raccoon at the garbage can — but frighteningly, not comically. She pushes her hair back from her clammy forehead and glares at him. 'Go *'way,*' she hisses. 'Get *lost.*'

Twenty-one

Arun is making his way back from work at the library; it has been a long day there and now his feet are dragging along alternately through grass and dust on the verges of the highway. He has missed the last bus to Edge Hill again. Cars swish by every second; everyone is on their way home, fanning out into the great wilderness of suburbs for their evenings around the grill or before the TV. If he were not also, in one sense, joining them, he might have felt trapped in the web of life through which he struggled.

But now it is not a car coming too close to the verge that makes him shrink, but the sound of thundering feet pounding closer, then overtaking him and passing him by. The jogger raises his hand and, without turning his head, shouts, 'Hi.' It is Rod, in his jogging briefs, his luminous headband, bare-chested, and in enormous white jogging shoes. The figure slows, comes to a kind of halt, knees still pumping, feet still lifting and pounding but in one place. Rod has stopped, for Arun. 'Hey,' he says, panting, the sweat pouring from under his headband down his rufous face. 'Come jogging?' he pants.

Nervously, Arun shakes his head, then smiles to show he means no offence: the idea, in one sense glamorous and flattering, of jogging beside the transcendent Rod, is too fanciful to be entertained. There is no way that a small, underdeveloped and asthmatic boy from the Gangetic plains, nourished on curried vegetables and stewed lentils, could compete with or even keep up with this gladiatorial species of northern power. 'Ehh — not today,' he stutters, shaking his head as if in shame.

Rod gives a good-natured nod that makes his reddish hair fall over his headband onto his forehead, like a horse's lick. 'Okay,' he agrees, 'another time,' and raising his hand in midair, jogs off alone, along the grass verge, towards the ripe sun and the horizon arched over the hill. Arun watches him meld into the radiance and is once more confirmed in his own shadowiness by the dust through which he trudges in his dusty brown leather shoes.

When he gets back to the house, Rod and his father are sprawled across the plaid cushions of the sofa in front of the television screen. Arun sees their outstretched legs and their uptilted shoes before he sees anything else in the dim light from the screen: Rod's sneakers heavy with dust, Mr Patton's well polished office brogues and diamond-patterned socks. Later, he makes out the beer cans on the floor beside them, and the baseball match that is being played on the screen, small agitated figures in white crouching, leaping and running for their lives — a cartoon version of combat. He hesitates by the door, wondering if he could go in — the scene is so convivial, so inviting, and the salt smell of tacos tickles his taste buds. But having rejected Rod's earlier overture, he knows he cannot expect it to be repeated: life deals in singles, not doubles, essentially.

Mrs Patton is washing bean sprouts in a colander at the kitchen sink; they spill over and scatter across the draining board. She gives Arun a conspiratorial smile. 'It's the big game tonight,' she tells him. 'They're eating a TV dinner. Shall we have bean

sprouts together? I thought I'd steam them.'
She shakes the colander and it drips onto
the floor.

Arun finds himself nodding since he
cannot convey to her what he would give to
join the two men in the den instead; he can
hear the cracks and cheers of the game, the
pounding of cushions and the shouts of
monumental approval and pain.

She notices. 'Oh dear,' she says bleakly,
'maybe you don't like bean sprouts?'

What can he say?

'Then we won't have them,' she says decisively and, folding them all up in her hands,
thrusts them into the garbage disposal unit,
stuffing them in so forcefully that she might
be angry. Arun is alarmed, but then she
turns around with a cloudless smile, inviting
him to cook an Indian dinner for himself.
'That's what you must be missing,' she says,
and begins to line up the bottles and packets
of spice, the jars and boxes of lentils and rice
that she has so painstakingly collected for
him.

There is nothing for it but to take the lentils she discovered in a health food store
from her hands and sift the small seeds
through his fingers, wondering what is to be
done with them. He has an urge to spill
them across the table, and leave them to

Mrs Patton and run. Down the grassy verge, up the blazing slopes, out of the town, into the next one, out of that and along the endless highways that ribbon through the state, through the continent. But, looking out of the window, he catches sight of the woods there, the leaves in their summer exuberance creeping up, rank and riotous, green and grasping, closing in. He can feel their damp stir of breath on his face, the rankness of compost.

He turns on the faucet and runs water over the lentils, washes them. With Mrs Patton watching, admiringly, he sets the pot on the stove and adds the spices she hands him, without looking to see what it is he is adding. Their odours are strong, foreign — they should be right. They make him sneeze and infect him with recklessness: he throws in some green peppers, a tomato, bay leaves, cloves.

'Is it the way your mother made it?' she blinks and asks when steam begins to rise and enfold them in smells not altogether appetising.

He cannot tell her that he has never seen his mother cook; she would understand that to mean that he never ate at home but starved, and at the moment he has had enough of her compassion. He merely nods and stirs. His glasses become fogged with the grease of turmeric-tinted steam.

'Now if more Americans ate that food, we shouldn't be making ourselves so sick — with heart disease and cancer and — and dreadful diseases all due to a terrible, terrible diet,' she says.

'Americans are very healthy people, Mrs Patton,' he says, 'more healthy than Indians.'

'Oh, shoo, don't you believe that. Just ask me about American health — I'll tell you,' she cries. 'The statistics are just awful. You go into any doctor's clinic and you'll see things that'll astonish you. We don't know how to eat,' she repeats. 'We've got to learn.'

It happens that just when he has poured out the lentils into a dish to eat — khaki-coloured, lumpy, at the same time thick and runny — Melanie walks in, back from school, carrying her book bag on her back like a sack of stones. She pauses as if she cannot believe what she sees, and stares — with increasing indignation — at the lentils dribbling out of the pot and into the bowl.

'Yuck!' she exclaims finally, the word exploding out of her like a bubble of masticated gum. 'What's *that?*'

'Melanie!' her mother cries. 'It is Ahroon's dinner. Ahroon cooked it. Please do not make rude sounds about what you know nothing of. I do believe you don't know what cooking is any more. Cookies and candy bars and peanuts is all you ever will eat but please don't make offensive remarks about other people's food.'

'Eeeuuuh, you call that food?' Melanie asks furiously, as if outraged by the very idea. 'I call that shit!'

She slams her book bag onto a chair and walks out, hunching her shoulders like a pugilist, while her mother's reprimands follow her out of the room.

Arun sits in front of his bowl of dhal. He stares at it, nauseated. He quite agrees with Melanie: it *is* revolting. He would much rather chomp upon a candy bar than eat this. But Mrs Patton comes and sits by his side, commiseratingly, coaxingly. She smiles a bright plastic copy of a mother-smile that Arun remembers from another world and another time, the smile that is tight at the corners with pressure, the pressure to perform a role, to make him eat, make him grow, make him worth all the trouble and effort and expense. Mrs Patton's smile contains no hint of pressure, it is no more than a mockup. Gently, it flashes a message as if on a flickering screen: 'Eat. Enjoy.' Helplessly, he does.

★ ★ ★

When he finally gets away from the kitchen and goes upstairs to his room, Melanie is sitting on the landing as if to intercept him. She does not move her legs out of his way and he steps over them gingerly. As he does so, he sees her lap is full of Hershey bars. She has eaten some of them, and she crackles the empty papers in her hands as he passes, again as if to draw attention. He is reminded, fleetingly, of beggars on Indian streets and the manoeuvres required to step past them on crowded pavements, their strategies to prevent this.

Unexpectedly, she speaks. 'Had your dinner?' she asks, with heavy malice.

He fights the urge to flee to his room and hide. He mumbles, 'Will you not have any? Aren't you hungry?'

She opens her mouth wide so he can see the sticky brown stuff of the candy adhering to her square teeth and stretching webs across her tongue. 'I'm so hungry I've got to eat this shitty candy,' she hisses. 'I can't eat that goo you and Mom cook down there,' she adds in bitter complaint.

He is consumed by both horror and contrition. He wishes to explain why the meal he had cooked had been so poor: it had been his first effort. He wishes to apologise for her having to eat candy instead. He is on the point of doing so when he realises it would mean a criticism of her mother, and so he desists. On the other side of the world, he is caught up again in the sugar-sticky web of family conflict. Desist, O desist. Edging past her towards his room, he gets away from her accusing glare.

Twenty-two

Mrs Patton, with her hand on the cart that
Arun is rolling as rapidly as he can along the
aisles of tinned soup, pasta and rice, tries to
slow him down. 'We haven't enough yet,
Ahroon,' she protests. 'You should have seen
the way I'd load a shopping cart when the
children were small. I'd have Melanie sitting
up here on the shelf, and there'd be such a
heap of groceries under her, she'd have to
stick her feet right up on top.'

Arun has seen mothers of young children
do precisely that — lift their babies onto the
collapsible shelf where they sit above hills of
cereal and cat food and diapers, usually
sucking the candy they have been given in
return for allowing their mothers to get on
with the shopping. He tries to picture baby
Melanie in the cart, queen of the groceries,

but what he visualises is a baby monster with elephantine legs.

'And do you know, that load wouldn't last us even a week. Three days and I'd be back for more,' she chuckles, hurrying to keep up with him. The wheels of the cart squeal, the rubber-soled shoes squeak, Arun swivels to avoid another loaded cart trundling past.

'Do they eat less now?' he asks. There is scarcely room in the cart for another package. He feels revulsion rising in his throat as if from too gigantic a meal.

'My no, they eat all the time,' she laughs, a little out of breath. 'But — but it's different now. We don't sit down to meals like we used to. Everyone eats at different times and wants different meals. We just don't get to eating together much now that they're grown. So I just fill the freezer and let them take down what they like, when they like. Keeping the freezer full — that's my job, Ahroon,' she declares, and grasps the handle to stop him so she can study the labels on the soup cans. Although he hardly felt that mealtimes at home had been models of social and familial gathering — Papa chewing each mouthful like an examiner on duty, Mama's eyes like bright beads, watching, his sisters perched in preparation to flap and fly, the only conversation permitted to do with the grim duty at hand: eating — there seems something troubling about the Pattons' system, too.

'Mushroom,' says Mrs Patton. 'You'd eat that, wouldn't you, Ahroon?'

He wants to point out that he is not her family. He considers saying something about Melanie's needs, the way she had flung them before him on the landing, making it impossible for him to ignore them. But he does not know how to bring up her name without leading Mrs Patton to think he was taking an undue interest in her. At last he says, 'But what about the rest of the family — do *they* eat it?'

'Oh,' she replies, tossing it into the cart and moving on, 'I told you, they take down what they like. Out of the freezer, you know. Or,' she adds vaguely because she is examining the cookies now, 'they make a sandwich. You see,' she goes on, with the faintest frown, 'what I cook, they don't like. And they don't like sitting at a table either — like you and I do,' she smiles at Arun with unmistakable significance, making him look away and redden.

'Counter number six looks free,' he mumbles, and trundles wildly away.

Twenty-three

Arun is jogging. With great deliberation he has folded and put away his spectacles, pulled on and laced up his newly bought sneakers, and now he is jogging. With the same deliberation and caution he jogs up Bayberry Lane, down Potwine Lane, along Laurel Way into Pomeroy Road. Amazed at his own daring, he jogs past lawns abandoned to the morning sun and past porches where old men sit, their baseball caps lowered over their noses, allowing the passing traffic to lull them into dusty sleep. He jogs past driveways where families sit expectantly around tablefuls of used clothes and shoes, carpet rolls and picture frames, table lamps and electrical gadgets, all surmounted by a sign saying *Yard Sale,* and other driveways where old ladies in straw hats prod with small trowels at beds of zinnias.

Still driven by resolve, he turns into Elm Street and jogs on past silent houses with rhododendrons screening their picture windows, under dense trees where wind chimes and hammocks dangle in the still air, and out onto Oak Street. His toes stub into his shoes, his ankles ache with the weight thrown on them, pain shoots up his leg muscles. He clenches his fists, and his teeth, and jogs on, hoping the barking dog will not break free of his chain to the dog-house, and that cars that roar their warning into his cars will swerve in time.

Sweat pours from under his hair onto his cheeks and runs down his chin. The heat of the still morning has a sullenness about it, the sparkle it had had earlier has dulled. He is slowing down. He is much slower now, tiring. But he will jog and jog — like Rod, like all those others; he has seen their contorted faces, their closed eyes, their shut expressions as they struggle to leave behind the town, the suburbs, the shopping malls, the parking lots, struggle to free themselves and find, through endeavour most primitive, through strain and suffering, that open space, that unfettered vacuum where the undiscovered America still lies —

Opening his eyes, Arun looks around

wildly to see if he has arrived. Just in time, for he is about to run into the low-dipping branches of forest trees that crowd the road along its upward slope, casting shadows like nets in the way of the unwary. It is not where Arun has meant to end. Lifting his feet heavily out of the dust, he plods on, and his shoulders are hunched now, his head is sinking lower. He must go further, further, and leave the trees behind, the smothering wilderness of them.

Cars are flashing by, dangerously close, forbiddingly silent and fast. He observes them with a kind of desperate appeal, willing one to stop and give him a ride, convey him quickly and efficiently to a given destination. Not one so much as slows down, the drivers clearly assured by his jogger's outfit that he has none.

Arun is dizzied by their passage; he gives his head a shake that sends beads of perspiration flying, and looks down at his feet pounding along the strip of dirt beside the road. Feet: he has never been so aware of their plodding inefficiency, their crippling shortcomings of design. He watches them come down in the dirt, lift up and boringly repeat their rudimentary action from which they seem unable to proceed or improvise, all the while aware of the chromium-centred wheels that flash past with mocking ease and smoothness, blowing insolent fumes back into his face.

The cars speed away like metal darts aimed into space by missile launchers in the towns they leave behind. Up at the top of the road, where it meets the interstate highway, they pause, then part as each makes its decisive movement towards its chosen destination. All along the highway there will be signs, shelter, food, gas stations, motorists' aid call boxes, Howard Johnson motels — everything for the convenience of motorists, the owners of the dream machines. Their passage will be easy, their destinations infinite. It is they, not the earthbound joggers, who are descended directly from the covered waggons and the trusty horses, who are the inheritors of the pioneer's dream of the endlessly postponed and endlessly golden West. They alone can challenge the space and the desolation, pit their steel against the wilderness and the vacuum, and triumph by rolling over it and laying it in the dust — contemptuously. In their sealed chambers, the drivers display their identities, their histories and their faiths in their windows for everyone to see and, with sacred charms dangling all about them, laugh as they plunge on, reckless.

The jogger only pretends. The jogger cannot even begin to compete. The jogger is overtaken and obsolete.

Arun stumbles to a halt at the top of the road, and sinks down on a dusty bank. A driver comes down on his horn in alarm, lets out a toot of warning, then whirls away. He is left sitting blinded by the dust and his own perspiration, nursing his knees and groaning at the thought of making his way back.

When he limps into the Pattons' driveway, he finds Mr Patton has just returned from work. He is getting out of his car, heaving himself out clumsily, holding a briefcase in one hand and a paper bag from the Foodmart in the other. 'Hi, Red,' he says to Arun. 'Here, will you hold this while I lock up?'

Arun puts out his hand and dumbly receives the bag damp from the seeping blood of whatever carcass Mr Patton has chosen to bring home tonight for the fire that will soon crackle its flames on the patio and send its smoke spiralling in at the open windows of the rooms where Melanie hides, where Mrs Patton bustles, where Arun will seek shelter.

Mr Patton locks up the car, emerges from the garage. They walk round the house to the kitchen door together. He asks, 'Where's everybody? Sitting on their butts in front of the TV? Doesn't anyone in this house do any work? That lawn could do with some cutting. Where's Rod?'

'He must be out jogging, Mr Patton,' Arun tells him, uncertain if this is an activity that Mr Patton approves of or not.

'Jogging, huh? Jogging. That boy spends so much time getting into shape he hasn't time left over to do anything with it.'

Mr Patton sounds tired, irate. Arun is wary and follows him into the kitchen where he puts the bag down on the table so he can leave quickly.

Mrs Patton, who has indeed been sunk deep into the cushions of the sofa, watching *Dallas* on television, struggles to her feet and appears, blinking. 'Oh dear,' she says, 'the freezer is full to the *top* with chops. I don't know that I want any more.'

Mr Patton ignores her. He is getting a can of beer out of the refrigerator. Opening it with a sharp jerk of his thumb, he demands, 'Where are the kids? Are they going to be in for dinner tonight? What have they been doing all day? Are they doing any work around here?'

Mrs Patton begins hurriedly to put away the chops. As she busies herself, she says,

'You know Rod's in training for the football team, Chuck. It's what you wanted him to do yourself —'

Arun knows when to leave a family scene: it is a skill he has polished and perfected since his childhood. He sidles out of the room and has his foot on the stairs when he hears them starting on Melanie.

'And Melanie? What's she up to? What's she in training for, huh?'

Arun needs a wash but Melanie has taken the cassette player into the bathroom with her and shut the door. The sounds of the saxophone and trumpets and a lead singer in distress are pounding upon the door, hammering it with all its fists. But the door stays shut, a slit of light beneath it. In between songs, Arun can hear, through his open door, water furiously rushing.

When she comes out, stumbling across the landing blindly, he looks up to see her passing the door, perspiration beading her clammy face. She can scarcely drag the cassette player along. Going into her room, she slams the door. He thinks he hears her crying but it could be the singer, in agony.

Rod is lying on his bed, amongst toy animals, music albums, comic books and dirty socks. He is bicycling his legs vigorously around in a giddily whirling motion that is however perfectly steady and rhythmic. His hands support his back and his face is contorted and inflamed.

Arun stands at the door, waiting till Rod's legs slow down and come to a halt. Then he says, with a slight cough, 'Uh, Melanie is sick, I think.'

Rod lowers his legs onto the bed. He lies there waiting for the blood to recede from his head, breathing heavily and evenly. 'That kid,' he grunts at last, 'just poisons herself. All that candy she eats. Won't eat a thing but candy. Anybody'd be sick.' He gives a snort that is both derisive and amused. 'Wants to turn herself into a slim chick. Ha!'

'By — eating candy?' Arun ventures, unconvinced.

'Yeah, and sicking it up — sicking it up!' Rod sits up abruptly, swinging his great legs onto the floor and planting his feet squarely on the boards. He bends down to pick at a nail. 'Man, she's nuts, that kid, she's nuts,' he mutters. 'That's all these girls are good for, y'know. Not like guys. Too lazy to get off their butts and go jogging or play a good hard ball game. So they've got to sick it up.' He straightens himself and sticks a finger into his mouth and wiggles it graphically. 'Can you beat that? Who'd want to be sick?' He gives his head a shake, then rises to his feet, straddles his legs and begins to swing his arms as rapidly as he had done with his legs.

Arun gets out of the way, quickly: one can't tell what is more dangerous in this country, the pursuit of health or of sickness.

Twenty-four

In the morning, he finds Melanie seated at the kitchen table, her chin lowered to her chest while her mother talks to her.

'Daddy thinks you ought to go outdoors and play games, Melanie,' Mrs Patton says as she cooks eggs. 'You have such a bad colour. You're not sick, are you, dear?'

Melanie does not raise her chin or answer. Arun, finding it is too late to retreat, tries to pour himself some milk and cereal as quietly and unobtrusively as he can. He sits down to eat it, painfully aware of the crunch and crackle, wondering if he should grasp the moment and tell Mrs Patton that Melanie is sick all the time, that Melanie spends her days vomiting in the bathroom. Melanie's face across the table looks like blotting paper that has soaked up as much water as it can hold: it is blotchy and discoloured; it sags. Does Mrs Patton not see?

Mrs Patton brings the saucepan of eggs across to the table. She starts spooning it out onto Melanie's plate, saying, 'Just plain scrambled eggs, dear, they'll do you good —' when Melanie violently pushes the plate away, gets to her feet and begins to cry.

'Why, Melanie, *dear!*'

'I hate scrambled eggs! Why don't you *ask* me what I want? Why can't you make me what I *want?* What do you think we all are — garbage bags you keep stuffing and stuffing?'

'Melanie!' Mrs Patton is scandalised. 'All I'm doing is asking you to eat a little scrambled egg —'

'I won't eat *anything* you cook. You can give it to the cat. Give it to *him!*' She points dramatically at Arun. 'I'm not going to eat any of that poison. Everything you cook is — poison!' she howls, and blunders out of the room, leaving her mother white with amazement.

Arun sits frozen in his chair: it does not seem right to continue with his breakfast but, after a moment, Mrs Patton gives a little shaken laugh and says, 'Poison! Did you hear that? What's gotten into her? What can she mean? My family is just so *strange.*

Now you'd never say that, Ahroon. *You* know it's nothing of the sort.'

He has no alternative then but to eat.

A little later she is jiggling the car keys. 'Ahroon,' she calls up the stairs. 'It's shopping time!'

He comes out on the landing and holds onto the banister, looking down at her gravely. 'Mrs Patton,' he says, 'I think we should finish the food in the freezer first.'

She stares at him in astonishment. 'Finish the food in the freezer?' she repeats. 'What an idea! Whyever should we do that? What would we do in an emergency? Come on, off we go,' she sings, rattling the keys more loudly, in a manner undeniably peremptory.

The white Honda Civic carries them smoothly over the trail of tar that lies melting in the blaze of the summer sun. The suburban houses with their screened porches on which old men sit dozing, their yards mown by tirelessly vigilant power lawnmowers, the booths of flowers and vegetables that bear cryptic signs — *Mums* and *Cukes* — the garages overflowing with old furniture and obsolete garden equipment, give way to fields of wildflowers — streaks of yellow, crimson, orange, hot vivid colours woven in with grasses — and of corn, ripe and glittering a gun-metal blue in the hot noon light all the way to the horizon where the forest stands a solid blue-black. Arun still finds it disconcerting to find, in this setting, the sprawling car park of the shopping mall into which Mrs Patton glides with accustomed ease. She parks the car amongst all the others that lie roasting in the sun, and leads the way into the Babylon of plastic plants, fountains constantly recycling water, artificial odours of vanilla and chocolate, children in strollers stupefied with ice cream and candy, and old people slumped on benches as if gloomily waiting for the show to begin.

Mrs Patton makes her purchases, Arun escorting her and following her with her bags. She seems tense, makes errors, cannot remember where the aisle of socks and stockings is, then forgets Rod's size. When they enter the Foodmart, she relaxes: it is as if she has come home. She tosses packets and cartons into the shopping cart lightheartedly. It is Arun who grows tense, finds his throat muscles contracting, tight with anxiety over spending so much, having so much. Wondering if this is how Melanie feels and if it is what makes her sick, he tries to persuade Mrs Patton to put back a carton of icecream from which she is reading out the label with a chuckle: ' "Our icecream is the best icecream. We know because we made it . . ." ' She is giggling but when Arun tries to take it out of her hands and put it back, 'I *want* it,' she cries, snatching it back. 'It's Chunky Monkey — my favourite.'

At the check-out counter he waits beside her while she leafs through a magazine full of pictures of pregnant starlets, babies born with two heads, and prisoners on Death Row. A young man in front of them who wears a T-shirt that says *Give Blood. Play Rugby* tosses packages of potato chips and nachos, jars of mayonnaise and mustard onto the counter for the girl to check.

'Settlin' in for the weekend?' asks the check-out girl who wears a jaunty jacket of red and white stripes and a red bow tie around her white collar. She snaps her bubble gum as she makes out his bill.

'Nah. My girl friend's bringing her parents to dinner. I'm gonna cook for them,' he explains. 'I've been cleaning the apartment and now I'm going to go home to cook the dinner.'

'Gee,' she says tonelessly, 'that's awesome.'

It is Mrs Patton's turn next and Arun helps her arrange all her purchases on the counter for the girl to check. Having made out a bill so long that it curls around her hand, she suddenly eyes Mrs Patton with close interest and demands, 'You pregnant?'

Arun is so startled that he steps backwards and flushes crimson. Mrs Patton is brought to a halt. 'At my age?' she cries.

The girl is not disconcerted. She goes back to snapping her gum and feels for change in the change drawer. 'You aren't that old,' she assures Mrs Patton kindly, handing her some coins. 'You had that glow, y'know, the kind that pregnant women have. I see a lot of 'em here so I can just tell. Thought you had that glow, y'know.' Then she loses interest in Mrs Patton and turns to say, 'Hi,' to a young mother who has placed her baby on top of bags of diapers and rolls of toilet paper and is unloading her cart with half-moons of perspiration staining her pink T-shirt even in the cool of air conditioning. 'Kooky-koo,' the check-out girl says to the baby. 'Bet you're Daddy's darling.'

'It's a boy,' the tired mother informs her, 'and I'm a single parent.'

Mrs Patton and Arun silently wheel their loaded cart out to the parking lot. Arun helps her unload it; he cannot bring himself even to look at her. He sees her fingers trembling a little as she lifts out the heavy grocery bags.

When they have strapped themselves into the car seats which smell of scorched rubber and feel like sticky tar, she says in a dry, cracked voice, 'Did you ever hear anything so silly?'

Arun shakes his head but dares not speak.

'That girl — she's just the silliest creature I ever met. Can you beat it?'

Mrs Patton is driving too fast. The car is veering in and out of the traffic dangerously. 'I mean, do I *look* pregnant?' her voice rises in anxiety. 'I'm not *fat*, am I, Ahroon?'

He shakes his head and mumbles. She is not fat, only shapeless. The slacks and T-shirts she habitually wears divide her shapelessness into different segments and bring them together in a piece that is so lacking in singularity that it is surprising it would occur to anyone to comment on it.

The car bounds forward as if it were being chased. Mrs Patton gives a strange little laugh. 'Or young,' she adds, 'am I? Ahroon?' then swerves suddenly to avoid the bumper of a loaded pick-up van she has ignored till the last possible second. It bears a sticker that says *Like My Driving? 1800-EAT-SHIT* and its driver lets out a loud hoot of warning.

Arun finds himself saying shakily, 'Slow down, please, Mrs Patton.'

Twenty-five

Summer is beating at them, out of a sky so blue that it threatens to spill and flood the green land. The horizon blurs, watery.

Arun wakes earlier and earlier till he feels he hardly sleeps. The window is too bright, too impossible to darken or ignore. A bird shrieks and shrieks in the top of the maple tree, its voice harsh and jagged. He tries to be quiet in his room, not to disturb the others who breathe invisibly around him. He walks barefoot into the bathroom and back. He dresses in clothes as light as he would in India. His eyelids are already heavy with the weight of heat and sleeplessness.

He goes downstairs with the cautious tread of a burglar. He pours himself orange juice, not wanting to make a noise with cup or kettle. The cat, who has spent the night outdoors, comes up to the window and sits amongst the laurels, watching him with a predatory air. The house rings with emptiness. Has everyone left already, or are they asleep?

When he returns from the library, Mrs Patton is there. He has to walk past her because she is sitting in the yard, in a deckchair. Her eyes are covered by large dark glasses. She is wearing clothes so minimal that they cover only a few inches of her chest and hips. The rest of her flesh is bared to his gaze. It seems to be frying in the sun because she has spread quantities of oil over it — a large bottle stands beside her in the grass — and it gleams brown and shiny. Her feet in sandals are stretched out in front of her: she has painted her toe nails a startling crimson. She breathes in and out deeply as if she were asleep.

She might have been on display in the Foodmart, a special offer for the summer, gleaming with invitation. Almost, one feels, one might see a discount sign above it.

Arun hopes to get past without being heard but his shoes crunch upon the gravel and she stirs instantly, lifting her head to gaze at him. She takes off and waves her glasses at him with an unfamiliarly expansive manner.

'Ahroon!' she calls. 'Hi! I'm sunbathing, Ahroon.'

He would like to disappear. He does not even want to glance in her direction. It is like confronting his mother naked. When he glances, as he must, he cannot help staring at her limp breasts that fall into pockets of mauve plaid cotton, freckled and mottled like old leather. Or at the creases and wrinkles cut into the slack flesh of her bared belly, grey and soft as if cut into felt. Mrs Patton, *why?*

He croaks, 'Hi,' and hurries past, but hears her sing out, 'Oh, Ahroon, you should try this. The sun's glorious! It just irons your troubles right out!'

When he bursts into the kitchen, his face purplish from the strain of all his turbulent feelings, he finds it is no longer empty either. Melanie is seated at the table in much the same costume as her mother's although in her case it is much more fully packed and filled. Her bare legs are locked around the chair legs and her face is lowered, along with strings of hair, into a tub of icecream which she is rapidly spooning out. It is the Chunky Monkey her mother bought. She stops when Arun enters and holds the spoon suspended, a globule of yellow cream slipping up her fingers.

Instead of looking away disgustedly as usual, she gives him a strange grimace. 'D'you see Mom?' she asks.

Arun does not understand immediately: he still finds it difficult to follow Melanie's slurred speech. While he turns over the sounds in his mind and tries to reconstruct them as words, the icecream slips off the spoon and onto the tabletop.

'She's *sunbathing!*' Melanie spits out suddenly, with great force, the same force that is pent up in Arun and that he will not allow to burst out.

He stares at her to see if her feelings really reflect his, but he cannot decipher her expression. It is certainly not the sullen mask he usually sees, but it is not one he can recognise.

Unexpectedly, Melanie grins. 'She won't be cooking you dinner tonight,' she says vengefully, then returns to the tub of icecream and attacks it with renewed ferocity.

Then Arun does see a resemblance to something he knows: a resemblance to the contorted face of an enraged sister who, failing to express her outrage against neglect, against misunderstanding, against inattention to her unique and singular being and its hungers, merely spits and froths in ineffectual protest. How strange to encounter it here, Arun thinks, where so much is given, where there is both licence and plenty.

But what is plenty? What is not? Can one tell the difference?

Hungrily, Melanie is eating the icecream. Her lips part so she can cram the spoon in, loaded and dripping onto her chin, then diving down for more, and more, of the sweet, sticky, dribbling stuff with which she needs to satisfy herself.

In a little while, Arun knows, she will be blundering upstairs when it will come streaming out of her, rejected.

Mrs Patton no longer cooks dinner for Arun. She does not set out to fetch food for her family either. She seems sunstruck, bedazzled, as she spreads herself on the sagging canvas of a deck chair, or sometimes on an immense towel laid on the grass, rousing herself only to tip more oil from a bottle into the cupped palm of her hand and smear it over her shoulders, her legs, her neck, the backs of her arms and her elbows. She does this with a slow, voluptuous motion — up, down, up, down — caressing the limp, lined flesh tenderly. The dark glasses she wears mask her expression as she does so. She looks up only when she hears someone leaving or entering the house, calling out a lazy, 'Hi! Come and enjoy the sun?'

The very idea appals Arun, if it means the baring of flesh in public. He has never seen so much female flesh before. Then to see it scarred and wrinkled, shrunk or sagging with age fills him not so much with disgust as with distress. His body shrinks and closes upon itself, affronted. Averting his eyes, he tries to slip past unnoticed.

Mr Patton clearly disapproves too. Slamming the car door and making his way around to the kitchen, he grumbles, 'Aren't you through sunbathing yet?'

'Mmm-hmm,' she answers gaily.

Mr Patton goes indoors, gets himself a can of beer from the refrigerator, and slumps onto the sofa in front of the television.

There is a kind of desolation in the kitchen now. Where once there had been so much bustle and activity, such ambitious brews and novel odours, there is now only a litter of empty jars and cartons that have been opened and emptied by various members of the household when hunger has overtaken them, then abandoned on counters and tabletops in ruined attitudes.

Arun, left to his own devices, finds he has

lost his appetite. He stays longer in town, getting himself a cheese sandwich from the deli and sitting on a bench under the huge dusty maple trees in the town square to eat it before going home. On other benches young couples sit on each other's laps, tightly interwoven. An old man goes about with a thin stick, turning over leaves as if he expects to find something underneath. A young man with his hair wrapped in a red scarf plucks at a guitar, drawing out melancholy notes that fill Arun with a canine urge to howl. Once he wanders into the cinema and sits among the popcorn eaters, suffering through a film about a large rabbit that enters the world of human beings and proves their equal. On shuffling out, he runs into one of the Indian students at the university. They are embarrassed at finding each other at such a show, alone. The others in the group have gone on a trip to Washington, he learns, to look at the sights. They will not be back till all the students return, on Labor Day in September.

It is difficult to believe that the hands of the Town Hall clock will move forwards, and the calendar on the brick wall behind the counter of muffins and doughnuts in the deli will lose it pages, one by one. The summer seems arrested in the sky, stalled in its great blaze of heat, too dispirited to move. The trees wilt, dust weighs down their leaves that have achieved full span and can unfold no further.

At dusk, he makes his way reluctantly the long miles to Bayberry Lane, past darkened yards where the smoke spiralling up from all the barbecue fires smells of charred flesh, of food that is spoilt. Cicadas rasp relentlessly and mosquitoes come swarming out of the woods, out of the wilderness. It was there all the time, waiting — and it is what has taken over the town, the household, Mrs Patton.

Twenty-six

Another morning, feverish with heat. The glare, pouring in at all windows, beats down upon the faded rugs, shows up dust where no one has cleaned.

But today Mrs Patton is in the kitchen. She is still in that mauve plaid sunsuit of hers, and the blue sandals, but at least she is on her feet, and working at the kitchen table. Perhaps there will be a return to normalcy now. Then she shatters such hopes by throwing Arun her newly roguish smile. She wears lipstick now, very pink. She is not very skilled at using it: it smears her front teeth. 'There you are!' she cries, too loudly. 'Come along! We're going to spend the day down at the swimming hole. It's too hot to lie in the yard and Daddy won't get us a pool, so Melanie and I've decided —' she looks archly through the door towards the den '— we'll go swimming instead, all by ourselves. Coming?'

It is Saturday. Arun cannot plead work. He stands despondent, and when Melanie comes to the door, dressed in her bathing suit with a big shirt drawn over her shoulders, and stares at him challengingly, he starts wildly to find excuses.

Mrs Patton will not hear them. No, she will not. Absolutely not. So she says, with her hands spread out and pressing against the air. 'No, no, no. We're all three of us going. Rod and Daddy have gone sailing on Lake Wyola and we're not going to sit here waiting for them to come home — oh no.'

Arun must go back upstairs and collect his towel and swimming trunks. Then he follows Melanie to the driveway where Mrs Patton is waiting with baskets of equipment — oils and lotions, paperbacks and dark glasses, sandwiches and lemonade. With that new and animated prance galvanising her dwindled shanks, she leads the way through a gap in the bushes to one of the woodland paths. Melanie and Arun follow silently. They try to find a way to walk that will not compel them to be side by side or in any way close together. But who is to follow whom? It is an awkward problem. Arun finally stops trying to lag behind her — she can lag even better — and goes ahead to catch up with Mrs Patton. He ought to help carry those baskets anyway. He takes one from her hands and she throws him a radiant, lipsticked smile. Then she swings away and goes confidently forwards.

'Summertime,' he hears her singing, 'when the living is eeh-zee —'

They make their way along scuffed paths through layers of old soft pine needles. The woods are thrumming with cicadas: they shrill and shrill as if the sun is playing on their sinews, as if they were small harps suspended in the trees. A bird shrieks hoarsely, flies on, shrieks elsewhere, further off — that ugly, jarring note that does not vary. But there are no birds to be seen, nor animals. It is as if they are in hiding, or have fled. Perhaps they have because the houses of Edge Hill do intrude and one can glimpse a bit of wall here or roof there, a washing line hung with sheets or a plastic gnome, finger to nose, enigmatically winking. Arun finds the hair on the back of his neck begin to prickle, as if in warning. He is sweating, and the palms of his hands are becoming puffy and damp. Why must people live in the vicinity of such benighted wilderness and become a part of it? The town may be small and have little to offer, but how passionately he prefers its post office, its shops, its dry-cleaning stores and picture framers to this creeping curtain of insidious green, these grasses stirring with insidious life, and bushes with poisonous berries — so bright or else so pale. Nearly tripping upon a root, he stumbles and has to steady himself so as not to spill the contents of the basket.

As he stands panting to recover himself, Melanie comes up the path, chewing on a grass, her brow lowered and surly. In the dim light under the branches, her face looks not only puffy but raw and swollen, the skin a mass of pimples. Throwing him her most contemptuous look, she strikes off the path, ostentatiously refusing to pass by him. He wants to yell, 'Melanie!' and demand her company, demand attention, but restrains himself and continues along his way.

Then the ground begins to slope steeply. He has to concentrate on how to lower himself downhill without dropping the basket. He places his feet carefully in the rungs of tree roots, frowning with anxiety over the difficult descent.

Below lies the swimming hole. Mrs Patton has already reached the shore. She, stands on a boulder, striking a pose. Then she looks back, laughing. 'Nice, Ahroon?'

'Very nice,' says Arun, miserably. He is pouring now with sweat and needs a swim, but it is something he never enjoyed at school, in the scummy green swimming pool that stank of boys, and in all his life he has never swum in a pond. He wonders if it is clean. He wonders what animal life might lurk in it. He cannot help eyeing it with the greatest suspicion.

The water sparkles innocently, spreading itself in a rough circle between rocks and overhanging pines. Mrs Patton has brought them to a sandy shelf where there are no other picnickers or swimmers; these all swarm at the other end of the pond, near the parking lot. Bare bodies gleam in the shimmer of heat on the sand. Relatively few of them are in the water: a knot of small boys, splashing, a dog effortfully keeping its head above the skin of water while its paws paddle invisibly underneath, a girl on a raft who seems asleep as she drifts. But the people on the beach make such a din — playing with rubber balls, turning up the volume of their radios — that it gives the impression of being crowded. This, too, makes Arun pause: he had not expected people at all. He would prefer there to be no one to witness him gingerly confronting the water.

Melanie has come out of the woods behind them and flung herself on the sand in a moody heap. Pulling candy bars out of a bag, she begins to unwrap them and bite at them angrily. Mrs Patton sighs, 'Dear, there are sandwiches in the baskets, you know.'

Arun stands at the edge, still wondering if it is safe to plunge in amidst the waterweeds that float thickly at their end of the pond (perhaps that is what keeps the other swimmers away). Then he becomes aware of Mrs Patton casually removing her sunsuit, slipping it off her hips and shoulders as she stands barefoot on a towel she has spread on the sand. Rather than see her stripped, he puts out his arms like a man fleeing and plunges hastily into the water, bracing himself for the cold splash, and falling on his stomach noisily and painfully just as he remembers doing all through his school years. Then he pushes away from the edge, through the dragging weeds to where the water is clear. He wonders if he has the strength to swim to the centre of the pond where there is a rock and a single twisted pine tree that seems to proffer shelter. He strikes out towards it purposefully but when he tires he turns on his back and lies on the water, kicking his legs mightily to give an impression of undiminished vigour. Now that he is contributing to the din, he begins to feel pleased. Surprisingly, it is due to the water, an element that removes him from his normal self, and opens out another world of possibilities.

Of course, he tires, and the knot of splashing boys seems suddenly close, threatening to overtake him. So he turns landwards again, breast-stroking with great gulps of air, and hopes that the green opacity of water will disguise his lack of stamina. He is relieved to crawl out onto the shingle, then upright himself on the sand. Bending over to pick up his towel, he glances surreptitiously at Mrs Patton's supine figure. She has put on her sunglasses and he cannot tell if she is sleeping: her lips are parted and the cords of her neck are relaxed, like slack ropes. Her body lies spread-eagled on the pink towel with another, smaller towel covering only those parts that Arun fears most to see. The rest of her straggles away from these points, limply. A small plastic radio by her head is playing: there is a fund-raising drive on for public radio and two young people are offering contributors coffee mugs and umbrellas if only they will ring in and send their subscriptions to 1-800-uh-uh-uh.

Melanie is gone. Where she sat there is

now a heap of candy papers, brown and gummy.

What is he to do? He has swum and swum. He does not want to be sitting beside Mrs Patton, both of them undressed, listening to the fund-raising drive. He moves away from her, up the sand, into the shade of the trees. Perhaps he can sit there on a tuft of grass, and it will be cooler. He wishes he had brought along a book. He dares not pick up the radio and take it with him; that would wake her.

But as soon as he settles himself upon the grass, the mosquitoes attack. Mosquitoes, midges, gnats, enough to craze anyone in search of peace. A few minutes, and they have got into his hair, his eyes, his nostrils. In disgust, he rises from the grass and goes deeper into the woods, hoping to leave the plague behind.

He is on another path. The earth is moist and crumbling under his feet. It seems to head somewhere. He follows it, parting the bushes and vines on the way, and comes to a clearing amongst some poisonous-looking plants with evil dark heads and a rank odour. Melanie is there, lying on the ground. Not on her back, not covered by a towel, but face-down in the dirt in which she has obviously been kicking and struggling. The dampness and discoloration around her show that it is not the strange green plants that give off that sour odour but her vomit. She is lying in her vomit, her hair streaked with it, her face turned to one side, and it is still leaking from her mouth.

'Melanie,' Arun whispers, 'Melanie — are you dead?'

She twitches and grunts, 'Hhh, hhh,' then rubs her face with her hands. It is smudged with dirt and soiled with vomit. Her eyes are tightly shut. 'Go. Go *'way*,' she bursts out, and thrashes her arms upon the ground. Then, with a groan, she lifts herself onto her knees, thrusts her finger down her throat and vomits again, copiously.

Arun backs away. He stands, his hands twisted at his sides, looking around to see if any help is coming. But the woods hold out nothing but these leaves, twigs, branches, fronds, roots and vines that he so distrusts. They murmur, menacingly, or perhaps it is the mosquitoes. Seeing no one, he approaches her gingerly — she is panting now, but still — and puts his hand on her shoulder. Its nakedness startles him and quickly he draws back.

'Melanie,' he says, desperately, 'shall I call your mother?' Staring at her, huddled on the ground and trembling, he feels this could be a scene in a film — a maiden at the feet of the hero, crying — but of course it is no such thing. It is not safely in the distance, flattened and reduced to black and white: it is daylit, three-dimensional and mal-odorous. They are not the stuff of dreams or even cinema: he is not the hero, nor she the heroine, and what she is crying for, he cannot tell. This is no plastic mock-up, no cartoon representation such as he has been seeing all summer; this is a real pain and a real hunger. But what hunger does a person so sated feel? He croaks, 'Shall I, Melanie, shall I?' but is rooted to the spot, its reality holds him captive. There is no escape, and it is Mrs Patton who comes in search of them and finds them.

'My Lord,' says Mrs Patton. 'Dear Lord.'

Twenty-seven

If summer was a gilded ball that had been flung up, up into the sky — high, high — now it comes plummeting down, down. It has reached its peak, it has hung for an incredible length of time, suspended in mid-air, but now the sun lowers itself, quite gently, with a barely audible sigh. The woods and meadows that had shimmered in its heat, now shiver and turn grey, subdued. Everything is normal again.

Families have returned from their vacation trips, but still wear their shorts to show their summer tans. Yellow school buses and the blue and white college shuttle service begin to trundle up and down the country roads again. The town is filled with returning students, all indistinguishably young and bright and laden with all the equipment needed to make their school year happy and profitable. Beer cans fly out of car windows and clatter along dusty curbs; music pounds with tribal rhythms. Shops have strung up banners saying *Welcome Back* and are preparing for huge sales of stationery, table lamps, wastepaper baskets and posters.

Arun has packed his belongings into the blue leatherite suitcase in which he brought them. He is puzzling over what to do with the parcel that has arrived from India only this morning, with its innumerable wrappings of brown paper and string, each bearing the mark of his sister's clumsy and impatient care, providentially catching him at the Pattons' before he moves out and back to the campus and the new room he has been allotted in the dorm, on the same floor as the other Indian students this time. The parcel contains a large packet of tea and a brown wool shawl, both calculated to help him through the coming winter. What has not been calculated is that he has no extra space for them in his suitcase: he is taking back precisely the same number of shirts, books and underwear as he brought with him, he has used up and thrown away nothing. The summer that had moved so slowly and laboriously has passed, leaving

318

no mark of its passage.

He picks up the box of tea in one hand, the folded shawl in the other. One is heavy, the other light. One is hard, the other soft. A lopsided gift. He holds them, trying to find the balance.

He glances across the landing. The door to Melanie's room stands open. He sees the white counterpane stretched neatly across the brass bed. He sees the bright mirror on the chest of drawers, a toy bear with a red ribbon propped against it. The room is empty. Melanie has left. She has been taken to an institution in the Berkshires where they know how to deal with the neuroses of adolescent girls: bulimia, anorexia, depression, withdrawal, compulsive behaviour, hysteria. (Mr Patton has taken on a night job to pay the bills.) They send in reports on her progress. She is playing tennis. She has helped bake cookies in the kitchen. She is making friends. She has gained weight. She can eat cereal, bread, butter, milk and boiled carrots without throwing up; she drinks hot chocolate at night. (Fortunately, Rod has won a football scholarship.) They find her compliant and obedient. With so much improvement, her family can expect her back soon. Not, unfortunately, in time for the new semester at school; that must wait a while.

Till then, the room stands empty, polished and cleaned, fresh and pleasant as it has never been while she occupied it. Mrs Patton has cleaned it herself, on her knees.

Arun goes downstairs to find her, the tea in one hand, the shawl in the other.

Mrs Patton no longer lies in the yard, sunbathing. The days are warm and still, with a silvery sheen, but she seems to have taken an aversion to the light, even to the outdoors. She no longer spends much time in the kitchen either. She has never offered to take Arun shopping, although the kitchen is drastically depleted, only remains left at the bottoms of jars and bottles. She dresses in skirts and long-sleeved blouses. She has voiced a tentative interest in traditional medicines; she talks of taking a course at the Leisure Activities Center in yoga, or astrology.

Once Arun heard Mr Patton growl, 'Here's another batch of catalogues come for you. What in God's name is numerology? Or gemology? Karmic lessons! What's that? Hell, what's this you're getting into?'

These catalogues, pamphlets and leaflets lie in drifts around her now as she sits on the porch, quite still, on an upright chair. She is holding an acupuncture chart on her lap but is staring over the top of it, through the wire screen, at the yard which is empty except for the cat carefully stalking a moth in a bed of dead and wilted flowers. Everything in that scene looks fatigued, spent or faded.

Arun goes quietly up to her. Too quietly because she gives a start and clutches her neck in fright.

'I'm sorry,' Arun apologises, clearing a frog in his throat. 'I — uh — brought you some presents. I'm leaving now, Mrs Patton.'

'Leaving now?' she repeats, bewildered.

'The semester starts tomorrow,' he reminds her. 'I've got to get back to the dorm. I'm packed.'

'Oh dear,' she says mildly.

'Please take these things — my parents sent them for you,' he lies, hoping they will never guess what happened to their gifts, and hands her the box of tea which she takes with a polite murmur of surprise. As she turns it over in her hands, studying the label with the habitual attention she gives to consumer products, she queries hopefully, 'Is it herbal?' Arun opens out the brown shawl. He shakes out the folds, then arranges it carefully about her shoulders. An aroma arises from it, of another land: muddy, grassy, smoky, ashen. It swamps him, like a river, or like a fire.

She looks at him, then at the wool stuff on her shoulders, in incomprehension. She picks at a fold of it, and sniffs. Slowly her face spreads into a flush of wonder. 'Why, Ahroon,' she stammers, 'this is just beautiful. Thank you, thank you,' she repeats, and puts her hands to her neck to hold the ends of the shawl together.

He withdraws quietly, going up to collect his suitcase and then finding his way out by the kitchen door, leaving her sitting on the porch with the box of tea on her knees and the shawl around her shoulders.

We hope you have enjoyed this Large Print book. Other Thorndike Press or Chivers Press Large Print books are available at your library or directly from the publishers.

For more information about current and upcoming titles, please call or write, without obligation, to:

Thorndike Press
P.O. Box 159
Thorndike, Maine 04986 USA
Tel. (800) 223-1244
     (800) 223-6121

OR

Chivers Press Limited
Windsor Bridge Road
Bath BA2 3AX
England
Tel. (0225) 335336

All our Large Print titles are designed for easy reading, and all our books are made to last.